Henry Laing Gordon

Dear Ryan,

All blessings on your 25th Birthday!

Hope this will be an interesting read, it is in
an older style with unusual chapter headings
to the modern mind, but skimming through
I thought some aspects of his life fascinating.

Yours,
Martyn
Dec 2019

CHAPTER I

Birth and Childhood. 1811-1825

The state of the healing art at Simpson's birth—Birthplace—Family superstitions—His father's bakery—His mother's Huguenot descent—Commencement of schooldays—Natural and antiquarian features of Bathgate district—The village hand-loom weavers as antiquarians and naturalists—His interest in Nature and craving for knowledge—Brothers' and sister's care for him—Size of his head—Village doctor's record of his birth—Schooldays cease at age of fourteen—Influence of his environment in developing his character.

James Young Simpson, who will ever be remembered as the discoverer of the pain-annulling power of chloroform, was born in the year 1811, at a period when there was room for a hero in the practice of the healing art in the British Islands.

It is true that in the seventeenth century Harvey had laid bare the great fact of the circulation of the blood and the practical Thomas Sydenham had swept aside the highly empirical systems and theories of medicine which had successively supplanted each other since Hippocrates first taught, and urged men to found their knowledge upon what they actually saw—on observation and experiment; and that in the eighteenth century men like Cheyne, Heberden, Cullen, and the wonderful Jenner had appreciably assisted in developing medicine at the same time that Hunter was raising surgery nearer to the level of a science. But even while Simpson was growing out of childhood all the powers of such professional giants as Bright, Addison, Abernethy, Astley Cooper, and Charles Bell, were insufficient to dispel the massive cloud of mystery and superstition which enveloped the practice of both medicine and surgery in this country and obscured whatever there was of truth in the teaching of these men.

In the first decade or two of this century the medical profession had not yet entirely abandoned the use of the golden-headed cane, nor had what Oliver Wendell Holmes calls the solemn farce of overdrugging yet ceased.

"Humours," "impostumes," "iliac passions," and such like were still spoken of—terms now heard only amongst country-folks in remote districts and that rarely, or encountered in curious old medical publications. Messes and abominations, prepared by the apothecaries according to more or less secret recipes handed down through the Middle Ages, were swallowed in good faith; blood-letting was still a panacea; and such remedies as that of holding a live puppy to the body for the relief of colic still had their professional advocates, but happily a decreasing number; whilst those pains

"... In the hour,

When the veil of the body we feel
Rent round us—while torments reveal
The motherhood's advent in power"

—pains which Simpson was the first truly to relieve by his application of anæsthetics, were gravely said to be alleviated by the swallowing of a concoction of white onions and oil. Surgery was no doubt ahead of medicine; but the early surgical records of this century have little more than a curious interest to modern practitioners. Operations entirely unknown to our professional forefathers less than a century ago are now performed in safety daily. Such mysterious diseases as "icteric irritative fever" and "acute sinking" after operations, dreaded then with the fear that is always inspired by unseen or ill-understood dangers, have vanished before the progress of modern science in which the introduction of anæsthesia was the first great step.

The practice of the branch of medicine which Simpson made so peculiarly his own—that of obstetrics—originally in the hands of women only, had been fiercely contested for by the two sexes during two centuries, and such was the feeling against man-midwives in Scotland that the dispute had scarcely ceased at Simpson's birth. The stronger sex, however, was then at last asserting its superiority, and to be an accoucheur was beginning to be considered after all as worthy of a gentleman. The despised art was preparing for its renaissance.

Simpson grew to manhood whilst science, aided by precise methods of accurate observation, was shedding new light upon physic, surgery, and

4

obstetrics. In fulfilling his great part in establishing the healing art on a firm scientific basis, Simpson encountered the full force of the ignorance and prejudice of his day both within and without his profession. It was, perhaps, fortunate that he was brought up in a small village and in a rank of life where he would meet from his earliest days with many superstitious beliefs and practices, strange and utterly irrational. A mind such as his would meet, reason, and experiment these out of existence. Probably through these circumstances he conceived the taste for archæology and antiquarian research which were his recreation in later years; but, what was more important, he gained also some training for the struggle with ignorance, untruth, and irrationalism, into which he threw with his eager vigour the whole strength of his manhood.

Simpson was born in the village of Bathgate, in Linlithgowshire, where his father, David Simpson, was the local baker. David's father, who died at the ripe age of ninety-one a few years after James's birth, was the descendant of a line of small hard-working farmers, who added to his work and his profit the practice of farriery. Although modern science has, by the aid of bacteriology, proved such practitioners of the rough veterinary medicine of the day to have been right in ascribing to unseen influences many of the diseases of animals which they found themselves powerless to check, the methods they employed for treatment when what they called witchcraft was at work scarcely have the support of present-day practitioners. In one of his addresses upon archæology Simpson records how his grandfather ordered and his own father took part in the burial alive of a cow in order to appease the evil spirit which was spreading the plague of murrain with fatal effect. And the older gentleman was known to have had more than one serious encounter with a witch. On one occasion an old beggar woman, who plied her calling in quite an original method—that of being wheeled in a barrow from farm to farm—hurled curses at old Simpson for ordering a servant to wheel her from his house on to her next calling-place, and vowed an awful vengeance on his family if he did not replace the servant with one of his stalwart sons. The farmer recollected that an ill event had followed the old woman's last visit, and quickly drew a sharp flint from his pocket and made a gash across her forehead with it. "Ah," he exclaimed, "I see what ye're noo, ye auld witch; but I've scored ye aboon the braith and my house is safe."

Simpson noted these and many other curious practices and beliefs, and afterwards pointed out in one of his addresses that they were probably, for the most part, relics of the pagan creeds and customs of our ancestors. He urged the making of a collection of the folk-lore of Scotland, ere it utterly disappeared before the march of modern civilisation, and suggested that, perhaps, some archæological Cuvier might one day be able to re-construct from these mythological fragments distinct pictures of the heathen practices, rites, and faiths of our forefathers.

In his early boyhood he listened to many stories of local and family superstitions told to him with all the earnestness of a firm believer by his father. He himself was the object of superstitious admiration to the simple villagers all through his boyhood, and they freely foretold great deeds from him in later years; for he was a seventh son, and the good luck which seventh sons were supposed to bring had appeared in the family soon after his birth. Up to the day on which James first saw the light, June 7, 1811, the baker's business had been going steadily from bad to worse, and the shop books showed that on that very day the lowest depths were reached. The baker, David Simpson, seems to have been curiously lacking in business method, although he was a hard-working man. But after James's birth he wisely interested his wife in his affairs, with the result that she energetically and successfully bestirred herself to recoup their fallen fortunes. Mrs. Simpson was directly descended from a fugitive Huguenot family, settled for many years on a farm near Bathgate, and intermarried with well-known families. Through her, indeed, Simpson claimed a distant relationship with the national hero, Sir William Wallace. The cares of her family and the strain of managing the increasing baker's business proved too much for her always delicate constitution, and she died when James was only nine years old. There is no doubt that the youngest child and favourite son had an unusually large share of his mother's society during those years; he was a peculiarly attractive child, "a rosy bairn wi' laughin' mou' and dimpled cheeks," and his manner, even when he was little more than an infant, was quiet and affectionate. When physical sufferings overtook the mother, the child's quiet sympathy and engaging manner helped and comforted her. Her own nature was bright,

6

vivacious, and energetic, quick to think and prompt to act; and she was full of love, sympathy, and piety. These maternal traits influenced the youth, and added a soft, refined—delicately refined—tone to the paternal influence, whence he received self-reliance and habits of persevering industry.

The boy's school-life began at the age of four years. The orthodox learning came very easily to him; he entered into both work and play so whole-heartedly that he at once became known as the "wise wean," and was at the same time ever sought after by his school-mates as a companion in out-door sports. The parish schoolmaster was one James Taylor, who had considerable ability for the post, and encouraged his pupils by kindly personal interest to develop affection for learning. But for Simpson there were other teachers and greater subjects for study in the countryside around Bathgate. The district was full of rich treasures for the field naturalist and for the antiquarian. Bathgate lies between the Firth of Forth and the Pentland Hills, in a geologically varied district, with a varied and abundant flora and fauna—more so in those days when Bathgate was a small village of hand-loom weavers than latterly, when it was a thriving little town, the centre of a coal, shale, and ironstone mining industry. The archæological features of the neighbourhood were full of interest. There was the famous "Catstane," of Kirkliston, which had puzzled antiquarians even before the establishment of the Scots Society in 1780, and at Kipps was one of the few remaining cromlechs—and that a ruined one—in Scotland; whilst the line of the Roman wall between the Firth of Forth and the Clyde was not far distant. There were traces of a Cistercian monastery founded by David I., and various hills and fields and caves were associated with the names of Sir William Wallace, Robert Bruce, and King Edward I.

Simpson thoroughly familiarised himself in boyhood with the natural features, as well as with the antiquarian objects in the district. He continued to investigate them during his vacations when a student at Edinburgh University, and rendered the neighbourhood famous archæologically by masterly monographs written when he was at the height of his fame. Amongst the village hand-loom weavers, a race of peculiarly observant and intelligent men, there were some who studied both the antiquarian objects and the natural history of Linlithgowshire. Simpson used to speak of one man, a daily labourer at the loom, who was able to write, in correct Latin, an accurate description of any plant or animal brought before him, although his earnings at the loom never amounted to fifty pounds a year. These men thoroughly enjoyed the evident interest of the "young philosopher" in their discussions and demonstrations, at the same time kindly directing his mind towards the simple, painstaking, true methods of observing and reflecting upon nature. There was no lack of change in his environment for him; his interest in natural phenomena was roused and kept alive during his drives round the countryside delivering bread to the farmers and cottagers, or in occasional visits to his parents' relations. He daily took his turn behind the shop counter, reading, writing, or drawing in the interval of waiting for customers. He trained himself to read or do his school lessons as readily in a roomful of romping children as in the quiet of the bedroom. It has been said that he never knew an idle moment from the day of his birth onwards, and his was such an indomitable and persevering energy that the remark is no exaggeration. But the pathway to greatness was made specially smooth for James Simpson. He was set upon it, and protected in his childhood, and guided in his youth, with the one definite object always in view. The Simpson family as well as the whole Bathgate community, took it for granted that eminence was to be his in whatever walk of life he entered seriously upon. His sister Mary and his brother Alexander looked upon him as a special care; the former watched over him as a mother, and the latter helped him in the ups and downs of boyhood, just as he constantly stood by him throughout the difficult days of his later career. It had always been a custom in Scots families of humble rank that one child, either from the exhibition of a natural aptitude, or through the ambition of the parents, was singled out to receive the advantages of a fuller education such as is within the reach of every able lad in Scotland. Honour and glory would thus be brought to the family, greatest of all if from the pulpit, while the less favoured members of the family would plod on in the same sphere of life as their parents. The world owes a great deal to the Simpsons, and particularly to Alexander, who cheerfully seconded their father's efforts to help forward their young brother, without a suspicion of jealousy. They knew he would be great some day, and therein they looked for their reward.

Happily there were ample means for all their requirements derived from the now prosperous bakery. The money was kept in one drawer, the till where the shop earnings were placed. All the household were free to draw thence supplies for their ordinary wants, James without stint; and he alone was exempted from the condition that he who profited must also contribute by the sweat of his brow. The boy took very full advantage of his fortunate circumstances and drank deeply of all the knowledge that came near and ever hunted for more. With each succeeding year the craving to know, and to know thoroughly, became more and more his ruling passion; by the time his schooldays were over it had gained complete mastery over him; happily for the human race Providence had so endowed him that when knowledge had come wisdom did not linger.

He was never in any way led away by the temptations that no doubt beset every boy in a village of hard-drinkers such as Bathgate was in his youth. Alexander took pains to warn him—"Others may do this, Jamie, but it would break all our hearts and blast all your prospects were you to do it," he said. It was not necessary to make appeals to James to work and fulfil the family predictions; he was as firmly determined to be great as they were sure he would be: He never forgot how much he owed to the loving help of his family, and to the fact that he was the youngest son growing up at a time when the family struggles were fairly over; when instead of its being an effort for the parents to provide the necessary funds for his education, the shop-till was well filled and the elder brothers and the loving sister were at hand eagerly willing to help. In student days when struggles came and the path seemed dark and beset with dangers, the knowledge of the firm faith in his powers of the family at home and of the scarcely smaller faith of the weavers, was a powerful incentive in the moments when he required any other than that of the spirit within him.

We cannot feel otherwise than thankful that up to the age of fourteen, when his schooldays ended, he had access to but a limited stock of literature wherewith to gratify his hunger for knowledge. To satisfy his appetite he was driven into the fields and the forests; every sense was stimulated, and became developed through repeated use. Thus he laid the foundation of his phenomenal faculty of rapid and accurate observation, and

9

of his no less phenomenal memory.

His imagination was fed with the legends of the district and tales of his remote moss-trooper ancestors told to him of an evening by his father. Though happily saved from being a bookworm to the exclusion of sounder means for acquiring knowledge, he devoured and digested every scrap of literature which came in his way. Like all Scots children of his class he learnt his Bible thoroughly from end to end—a knowledge which served him well in later years. Shakespeare followed the Bible in his own review of his favourite reading as a boy; but a gazetteer or an almanac was quite as acceptable. His taste was for solid fact—fact which he could learn and put to the test; thus the great open book of Nature was the attraction he most readily yielded to. But nothing in book form ever came amiss to him; if between the covers there was useful information to be had, Simpson extracted it and stored it away in his capacious brain.

The unusually large size of his head, a source of admiration in manhood, was in childhood an object of wonder to observers. In manhood he wore his hair in long locks, and this was apparently his habit in boyhood. Once a strange barber cut his hair so close that his brother took upon himself to go and rebuke the man. "The callant had suck a muckle head," was the retort, "I was doin' my best to mak' it look respectable." A close-cropped head gave altogether a too sportive appearance to the "young philosopher" in the eyes of the watchful elder brother.

There is no evidence that Simpson displayed in his schooldays any special leaning towards the medical profession; it cannot be reasonably urged that his grandfather's rough skill in the treatment of animals fostered any medical tendency in him, for James was but five years old when the old man died. Even had he been of an age to understand them, the methods employed would have scarcely recommended themselves to a youth of Simpson's nature, sufficiently to raise a spirit of emulation within him. It is also not recorded that the village doctor took any special interest in the boy or brought any influence to bear upon him; although his note-book thus gives the earliest record of the future prince of obstetricians:—

275.—June 7. Simpson, David, baker, Bathgate. Wife, Mary Jarvie. Æ. 40. 8th child, son. *Natus* 8 o'clock. *Uti veniebam natus.* Paid 10s. 6d.

James displayed his superiority so decidedly in the village school that when he reached the age of fourteen it was decided to send him to Edinburgh University without further waste of time. It was no unusual age for boys to commence their University career in Scotland. There was no secondary education in the Scots provinces, but instruction intermediate between that of the parish school and what is ordinarily known as University education was given within the walls of the University itself. Boys of humble rank who aspired to a profession were sent up, as indeed many still are, at the age of fourteen or fifteen, to attend these junior Arts classes in which this instruction was, and still is, imparted. The University was crowded with schoolboys of all ranks of life gathered together from town and country, and consisted of nothing more than a collection of class-rooms devoted to the giving of instruction in lecture form. This stepping-stone of junior classes threw open the higher education to hundreds of youths whose equals in England had no such advantage at that time. Scots University education besides being thorough was decidedly cheap, so that the church, law, and medicine received many recruits from the class out of which Simpson was drawn.

His environment up to the age of fourteen was well calculated to train him for the great work that lay before him. The legends of the district, and the sight of the objects of archæological interest which he came across in his rambles out of school hours, were powerful stimuli to his sensations; whilst the accurate observation of natural phenomena in field and hedge which the kindly interested weavers helped him to, was also a valuable educative influence. It is probable that his senses received much of the training which was to lead to his ultimately being the greatest physician of his day by these means, rather than from the instruction imparted to him in the village school, or derived by him independently from the books that came in his way. It was undoubtedly a fortunate circumstance that he was born and bred in an out-of-the-way country district, where he drew his lessons from Nature and the phenomena which lay round him, rather than in a great city where he would have been educated on the stereotyped orthodox system. When we look further back, asking why he saw sermons in stones and books in the running brooks, to which the bulk of his schoolfellows were entirely blind,

11

we are bound to confess that we find no satisfactory answer in his family history, to which it is customary to look for an explanation of such tendencies. Heredity played no great part in making Simpson great; from the paternal side there was imparted to him a vigorous physique; from his mother he received the bright, happy, sympathetic, and alert disposition, which descended through her from his French ancestors. He was provided with a brain of marvellous quality and phenomenal size. But it was the environment which acted upon this brain and brought out the capacities born in him without any apparent hereditary bias, and which might have remained entirely latent under less favourable circumstances. No small part of the development was due to the people among whom he lived; a race of men accustomed to rely upon their senses which were always with them, rather than upon books which they seldom saw, even if they were able to read them; and to observe not only all that lay around them, but also the characteristics of their fellowmen with whom they were brought into contact—the close contact of different classes which obtains in village and rural life. Simpson was taught to study Nature whether in field or fellow-creature first, and the knowledge and opinions of men as expressed in books afterwards.

CHAPTER II.

Student Days. 1825-1830.

Visit to Edinburgh—Sent to the University—Takes the Arts classes—Gains a bursary—Influence of MacArthur and Reid—Robert Knox the anatomist—The Burke and Hare murders—Superiority of the extra-mural teachers of the day—Edinburgh an intellectual centre—University life—His mode of living as a student—Apprenticed to a chemist—Studies surgery under Liston—Regularly falls asleep in the obstetric class—Influence of his teachers—Verse writing—Description of the medical student of the day—Vacation work—Death of his father—Obtains qualification to practice at the age of eighteen.

Although Edinburgh was only eighteen miles from Bathgate, Simpson visited it only once as a schoolboy; probably he walked all the way, for railroads were as yet unknown and it was not a long walk for a country-bred vigorous youth. He exercised his already formed habit of noting objects of interest during this great event in his boyhood, and in his journal there are copies of old inscriptions from tombs in the famous Greyfriars' Churchyard to which he made his pilgrimage.

The boy's nearest and dearest ambition was to become a student at "the College," as Edinburgh University was familiarly termed. It received encouragement in the periodical return to the village of elder boys who had gone up before him. He was specially struck, and afterwards stimulated, by the appearance of one John Reid, his senior by two years, and his former companion in many a country ramble, who came back for the vacations smartened up both physically and mentally by the new life.

Although the collegiate life characteristic of Oxford was unknown in Scots Universities, there was social intercourse amongst the boys very different from that of the village. The ancient Edinburgh University attracted students from all parts of the world, mostly for the medical curriculum, but many preceded the professional course with a year or two's attendance on the Arts classes; and it was usual for young Englishmen of good family to spend

13

a session at Edinburgh before going to Oxford or Cambridge. Probably before he entered the medical classes, Simpson rubbed shoulders with lads of all ranks from home and abroad. Pillans was at this time the Professor of Humanity, Wallace held the chair of Mathematics, John Wilson—better known as Christopher North—that of Moral Philosophy, and Dunbar was Professor of Greek. Wallace had begun life as a bookbinder's apprentice, and Dunbar had risen from being a gardener; the example of these men under whose influence he was brought encouraged the baker's son to go and do likewise.

The family had sent him off to the College with the mission to be famous, and he was beginning only in an orthodox fashion when he entered himself for the curriculum in Arts. It had been easy for him, with his magnificent brain power, to stand *dux* of the village school over the ordinary village youth; but here, in Edinburgh, he was brought into competition with the picked boys from other country schools, and intellectually eager youths from town schools where the course of instruction was such as more easily to lead to early University success than that of the Bathgate parish school. At first he found difficulty and desponded. The keen observer with senses all alert was dashed to find so much of the College life to which he had so eagerly looked forward only a magnified repetition of the dull school routine. But he was too intent on ultimate success to be repulsed by his initial disappointment, and soon brought his mind into adjustment with the circumstances he found himself in, reserving leisure time and vacations for the exercise of his faculties as he most loved to exercise them. He did not persevere in the Arts course after he found his tastes led him to other studies; he did not trouble to obtain the Master of Arts degree, which was then conferred in a very lax manner; probably he saw its worthlessness, for it was not until the passing of the Scots Universities Act in 1858 that this degree became really valuable. He recognised, however, the value of laying a good foundation of general knowledge; without straining after any distinction he acquitted himself creditably in all his classes. In the second year of the curriculum he won one of the numerous small bursaries of the value of £10 a year, for which logic was one of the chief subjects of examination; but as candidates were restricted to those who possessed either the name of the

14

founder, Stewart, or that of his wife, Simpson, the competition was not particularly severe. His individuality and natural straightforwardness attracted the attention of some of his professors. The boldness of his original essays provided them with food for comment in a manner dear to the professorial heart.

The Arts curriculum served him usefully in helping to develop a literary style and in teaching him how best to express his vigorous thoughts, as well as in strengthening his knowledge of Latin and Greek. According to the record preserved on his class certificates he worked attentively and diligently; but the mere fact that he did not excel is sufficient proof that he did not make an attempt.

During his Arts course Simpson lodged at No. 1, Adam Street, along with the John Reid already mentioned, who was now a medical student, and with a Mr. MacArthur, who had been a junior master at the Bathgate school, but had now also commenced to study medicine. MacArthur was a man of dogged determination; he urged Simpson to persist with his Arts course when his spirit seemed to rebel against it, and so long as they were together seems to have maintained some of the authority of the usher over both of the youths. The spirit of work was strong within him. Soon after Simpson joined him he related that he could then do with four hours' sleep, John Reid with six, but he had not been able to break in James yet. What MacArthur and the Arts course could not do, however, the attraction of medicine accomplished without effort, and Simpson soon formed the habit of early rising.

It seems remarkable that so much study should have been required when, compared with to-day, the science of the healing art was in but a rudimentary condition. The teachers of the day had, in spite of Sydenham, a great regard for authority, and burdened their students with much that is utterly unknown to the present generation, and, if known, would be regarded as worthless. A very large part of the curriculum consisted of practical and bedside work, so that book study was necessarily left to the evening or early morning. All three students, moreover, were fired with ambition, and thirsted for something more than mere professional knowledge. MacArthur constantly urged on his two young friends, and foretold great things for them if only they would work. When he afterwards heard of their successes he used

15

to say, "Yes, but *how* they worked." Simpson became the greatest living obstetrician, and Reid rose to be Professor of Physiology in St. Andrew's University. MacArthur never became famous; his name is known only because of the initial impetus which his influence gave to the professional careers of his two young friends.

In his close association with two such men as MacArthur and Reid, Simpson was again fortunate in his environment. The art of medicine was also fortunate inasmuch as at the right moment the right influences were at work to direct his mind towards it. While occupied in mastering the laws of hexameter and iambic or in assimilating the prescribed portion of Virgil and Tacitus, he happily now and then, living with two such enthusiastic medical students, got a taste of the more stimulating study of things scientific—food which was more agreeable to his mental palate, more suited to his mental digestion. By peeps into anatomical books, by little demonstrations of specimens in their lodgings, and by occasional visits to some of the lecture rooms or the wards of the Infirmary, his appetite was whetted for that great study of nature which his youthful training at Bathgate had prepared him for, and for which his mental constitution was specially adapted. One can picture the eagerness with which he would cast aside the finished Greek or Latin essay and urge the not unwilling embryo professor to demonstrate a bone or lecture on an anatomical preparation.

Sometimes as a special favour he was taken by Reid to hear one of the lectures of the notorious Robert Knox, the extra-academical teacher of anatomy, whose strong personality and unrivalled powers as a lecturer were at that time attracting to Surgeon's Square hundreds of students, while Munro (Tertius) was mechanically repeating his grandfather's lectures from the University chair.

It was towards the end of 1828, when Simpson was just about commencing his medical studies that Edinburgh, and in fact the whole of civilised Europe, was horrified by the revelation of the doings of Burke and Hare, when they were at last brought to justice for the long series of crimes perpetrated for the purpose of selling the bodies of their victims to the anatomical schools. Knox having a class of some four hundred students had special difficulty in meeting the demand for "subjects," and it was brought to light at the trial of Burke that the majority of the bodies were disposed of to Knox. As was only natural, a fierce indignation against Knox sprang up in the city. His residence was assailed and his effigy burnt. His life was in danger at the hands of the mob on more than one occasion.

Lord Cockburn in his "Memorials of His Time" says that all the Edinburgh anatomists incurred an unjust and very alarming though not an unnatural odium—Dr. Knox in particular, against whom not only the anger of the populace but the condemnation of more intelligent persons was directed. "But," he says, "tried in reference to the invariable and the necessary practice of the profession our anatomists were spotlessly correct and Knox the most correct of them all."

These were stirring times in Edinburgh medical circles. The strong, cool demeanour of Knox under the persecutions to which he was subjected, must have made an indelible impression on Simpson's mind, and the memory of it may have served to strengthen him in later years when himself subjected to the unjust accusations of thoughtless and ignorant people.

One night when Knox had attracted a large class to hear him on a favourite subject, the crowd in the street mustered in unusual force; the yells and howls from outside were heard distinctly in the class-room. The students got alarmed, and kept looking to the doors of egress. Knox perceiving the restlessness and alarm of his audience paused, and then addressed to them reassuring words, expressing his contempt for the cowardly mob, and reminding them of the great men who at different times had suffered persecution for the cause of their science. His statement was received with such cheers as resounded beyond the class-room walls and actually cowed the uproarious mob, so loudly did the students applaud the words of the man who, they knew, daily placed his life in danger in order to lecture to them, and whose last hour seemed to have come, so great and threatening was the crowd on this particular evening.

If Simpson did not actually witness such a scene as the foregoing—he was not a member of Knox's class until the session 1830-31—he must at least have known full well about it at the time, and shared with the whole body of students the worship of the man as a hero. His fellow lodger, Reid, was not only a distinguished pupil in Knox's class, but became one of Knox's demonstrators in 1833, and was always a prominent Knoxite. We know also that Knox went down to Bathgate to visit Reid's relations there, so that it is justifiable to conclude that Simpson came closely in contact with this remarkable teacher. That the relationship between Reid and Simpson was most intimate we have the former's own words for. At a public dinner given to him when appointed to his professorship in 1841, he said, "In the croupier (Simpson) I recognise my earliest friend, a native of the same village. We were rivals at school and at college. We stood to each other from boyhood upwards in every possible relation, whether of an educational, warlike, delicate, or social character, which the warm and fitful feelings peculiar to boyhood and youth can produce."

In the end Knox and Reid quarrelled over a scientific matter. Knox never recovered from the effect of the Burke and Hare incident; in spite of the favourable report of an influential committee appointed to inquire into his share in the proceedings, and his own explicit statements, the public never acquitted him of at least a wilful shutting of his eyes to much that ought to have aroused his suspicions. His crowded class-room gradually became empty during the next few years, and the once brilliant, talented, and determined man became demoralised and left Edinburgh. Christison says that Knox finally died almost destitute in London, and that one of his last occupations was that of showman to a party of travelling Ojibbeway Indians.

However the strong personality and attractive lecturing of Knox may have influenced him, it is undoubted that to the personal influence of MacArthur and Reid, acting upon his constant hunger to know nature and truth, stimulated as it was by what he saw of anatomy and physiology, we owe the fact that Simpson decided to enter the medical profession.

Although the number of medical students in Edinburgh University reached one of its highest points during the years that Simpson was a student, it is remarkable that with one, or perhaps two, exceptions, the University professors were men of no marked eminence in their various subjects. On the other hand, the extra-mural teachers included men of such wide reputation as Knox, Lizars, and Liston. Syme, who reached the height of his fame as a surgeon about the same time that Simpson became renowned, had just resigned the teaching of anatomy to take up surgery; shut out at first from the wards of the Royal Infirmary by jealous colleagues, he was boldly establishing for himself the little Minto House Hospital, which became the successful nursery of his own unsurpassed system of clinical teaching, and remains in the recollection to this day as the principal scene of Dr. John Brown's pathetic story, "Rab and his Friends." It was chiefly these extra-academical teachers who at that time made the medical school famous, and were raising for it a reputation in surgery such as it had acquired in physic in the days of Cullen. In certain subjects the students would, according to the regulations for the degree, take out their tickets of attendance on the professor's course of lectures, but would put in only a sufficient number of appearances to entitle them to the necessary certificates; the real study of the subject being made under the more accomplished teacher outside the University walls.

Edinburgh was at this period much more than the scene of the foremost medical and surgical teaching of the day in the world. It was a striking centre of intellectual activity. Sir Walter Scott, Cockburn, and Jeffrey were famous in literature and politics; Chalmers and Moncrieff in Church affairs; and Aytoun, John Wilson, Sir William Hamilton, and Sir David Brewster were names that attracted men from far and wide to the modern Athens. English and foreign advocates, scholars, artists, squires, and noblemen mingled together to hear or see some of these men. Lord John Russell, Henry Temple—subsequently Lord Palmerston—and Lord Melbourne were amongst the young Englishmen who attended university classes for a session or two; and H.R.H. the Prince of Wales, and his brother the Duke of Edinburgh, each matriculated in later days. When Simpson began his studies Knox was the great lion, without a visit to whose class-room no sojourn in Edinburgh was complete; just as in later years Simpson's house in Queen Street was the resort of all sorts and conditions of distinguished people.

The University had little control over her students once they were outside the gates of the quadrangle. There were no residential colleges; each youth found lodgings for himself suitable to his means, and led a perfectly independent life. So long as he conducted himself with propriety within her walls his Alma Mater cared little how he conducted himself or how he fared outside. Before 1858, when the Town Council controlled University affairs, there were sometimes attempts to order the comings and goings of students. It is recorded that in 1635 the Town Council discovered that the scholars of the College were much withdrawn from their studies by "invitations to burials," which "prejudiced their advancement in learning," and they enacted that no student was to be permitted to attend burials except those of University or city worthies. This was at a time when some of the students were provided with residences inside the University, but by the beginning of the eighteenth century College residence had ceased. From time to time attempts have been made to render the students conspicuous in the city by the wearing of red gowns, but without success; and those of all faculties continue to be their own masters, in marked contrast to the mode of government in force at Oxford and Cambridge. Recently, in the eighties, a batch of students who had figured in the police-court after a riot in the gallery of a theatre were surprised to find themselves summoned before the Senatus Academicus and rusticated for varying periods; this, however, was but a spasmodic exercise of power. The chief advantage claimed for this custom of leaving the student to his own devices is that it encourages independence and develops each man's individuality better than a system of discipline and control. In men of Simpson's calibre it certainly has had a good effect.

Although the family in Bathgate strained every nerve to keep James well supplied with the necessary funds as a student, they were not able to place him in such a pecuniary position as to make it unnecessary for him to exercise economy: He appears to have been very careful indeed of the money which he had; much more careful than when he reckoned his income by thousands. He kept methodical accounts of his expenses down to the most trivial items, and regularly submitted them to his family. His cash-book opened with the following quotation from a small book called the "Economy of Life," which figures at a cost of ninepence:—"Let not thy recreations be expensive lest the pain of purchasing them exceed the pleasure thou hast in their enjoyment"; and to this he added:—

"No trivial gain nor trivial loss despise;
Mole-hills, if often heaped, to mountains rise.
Weigh every small expense and nothing waste;
Farthings long saved amount to pounds at last."

It is easy to see here the imprint of a well-known national characteristic, from which, however, he completely shook himself free when prosperity came to him.

His share of the rent of the Adam Street lodging amounted to only three shillings a week. The entries in the cash-book show how frugally he lived and how every spare sum was devoted to the purchase of books. His library, the foundation of much of his encyclopedic knowledge, was a curious mixture. Adam's "Antiquities," Milton's Poems, Byron's "Giaour" and "Childe Harold," a Church Bible, Paley's "Natural Theology," Fife's "Anatomy," and "The Fortunes of Nigel," were amongst those entered as purchased. The daily entries were such as the following:—"Subject (anatomical), £2; spoon, 6d.; bread and tart, 1s. 8d. Duncan's Therapeutics, 9d.; snuff; 1½d.; Early Rising, 9½d."

He followed out the usual student's custom of the day of learning dispensing by serving for a time in a chemist's shop. The late Dr. Keiller, of Edinburgh, used to relate how, while he himself was so employed in a chemist's shop in Dundas Street, one day "a little fellow with a big head" was brought in and entered as a pupil by a relative. The little fellow was Simpson, and no sooner was he left in the shop than he sat down with a book upon drugs, and turning to the shelves took down drug after drug to read up. The prompt industry of the big-headed fellow deeply impressed Keiller.

James attended most of the University classes, but studied surgery under the great Robert Liston, the foremost extra-mural surgeon, daring and skilful as an operator and of great repute as a lecturer, who afterwards filled the post of Professor of Clinical Surgery in University College Hospital, London. Liston was an abrupt-mannered but sincere man, and a keen lover of truth. He was a warm advocate of hospital reform, and was successful in introducing several needed improvements into the Royal Infirmary after a fierce fight. Here again Simpson was brought under the influence of a strong, self-reliant man with a distinct tendency towards controversy; to whom he was also attracted by the fact that Liston was a native of Linlithgowshire. Liston and Syme, after being close colleagues, quarrelled most fiercely, and were bitter rivals until Liston removed to London in 1835. Simpson attended Liston's lectures during three sessions.

There is no record of his having obtained great distinction in any of the medical classes, but his certificates show that he worked with pre-eminent diligence in them all, and obtained a characteristic mastery of each subject. If any exception occurred it was in the very subject in which he afterwards earned his greatest scientific fame—that of obstetrics. He attended Professor James Hamilton's course of lectures on that subject early in his career, and apparently felt so little interest—the subject only became a compulsory one for examination for qualification in 1830—that he regularly went to sleep during the lecture. The excuse urged was that the lecture being a late one, three to four in the afternoon, it found him tired out after a long morning of study, lectures, and practical work. But had he been keenly interested he would have been wide awake, for Hamilton was a forcible, if plain, lecturer.

Hamilton was another of Simpson's teachers who exhibited the same uncompromising fighting characteristics—eager and strenuous in his efforts to obtain some object—which Simpson himself afterwards displayed. He fought hard for fifteen years to gain recognition for the subject which he taught, and to have it included in those necessary for qualification. He succeeded in the end, but in the course of the struggle had to bring two actions at law against professional brethren. In one the defendant was Dr. Gregory, whose teaching was mainly responsible for the British system of medical practice in the early part of this century, viz., free purging, free bleeding, and frequent blistering, and who was the inventor of that well known household remedy, Gregory's powder. Gregory was also a pugnacious man and could not abide the pretensions of the representative of the despised art of midwifery; he administered a public caning to him, and had to pay £100 in damages which, it is said, he offered to pay over again for another opportunity of thrashing the little obstetrician. This encounter occurred before Simpson became a student, but the memory of it was frequently revived in the subsequent disputes which Hamilton carried on.

The notes which Simpson took of the curriculum lectures were concisely made and full of comments, criticisms, and queries. He by no means bowed down to authority; he allowed nothing to pass which he did not understand at the time, and specially noted points which it seemed to him his teachers themselves did not understand.

Like most young men of his abilities and temperament, Simpson took pleasure in rhyming, and some of his verses are preserved. They indicate something of the rollicking spirit of the medical student's life seventy years ago. The medical student at that date has been described in a recent interesting sketch of Edinburgh student life as wearing a white great-coat and talking loud; his hat was inclined knowingly to one side of his head, and the bright hues of an Oriental handkerchief decorated his neck. There was a great deal of acting in his motions. He was first at the door of the theatre on a Saturday night, and regardless of the damages sustained by the skirts of his coat, secured the very middle seat of the fifth row of benches in the pit. Simpson, however, hardly conformed to this description. He enjoyed recreation as much as any man, and had a keen sense of humour which made him popular among his fellow students, but he was saturated with the love of study and was not led into extravagances of the Bob Sawyer type, or the harmless inanities of Albert Smith's immortal Medical Student.

During the long summer vacation he noted carefully his observations on the botany, zoology, geology, and even the meteorology of the Bathgate district. Dr. Duns, in his memoir, points out that he was much more at home with the phenomena of organic than with those of inorganic forms. His highest powers came into play when he had to do with the presence of life and its varied manifestations. Even his antiquarian notes illustrated this. He passed at once from the things to the thoughts and feelings of the men associated with them.

In the holidays he also assisted the village doctor in visiting and dispensing, and lent a willing hand in his father's shop when he was wanted, often enough driving the baker's cart on the daily round of bread delivery.

In January of the year 1830 his father was taken seriously ill, and James hastily left Edinburgh and tended him till his death. On his return he presented himself for the final examination at the College of Surgeons. This he passed with ease and credit in April, and found himself a fully qualified medical practitioner at the age of eighteen.

CHAPTER III

Further Studies. 1830-1835

Applies for a village appointment—Disappointment—Brother's help to further studies—Dispensary assistant—Obtains University M.D., 1832—Thesis—Assistant to the Professor of Pathology—Turns to obstetrics—Attends Professor Hamilton's lectures again—Royal Medical and Royal Physical Societies—Edward Forbes—The Oineromathic Society—Foreign tour—Visits Liverpool and meets Miss Jessie Grindlay—His characteristics, principles, and methods, with extracts from addresses.

There now came the first crisis in Simpson's medical career. After his father's death he felt that having obtained his qualification to practise it was his duty to relieve his family of the burden of supporting him through more extended studies. After due deliberation he applied for a small appointment which would have served as a nucleus for private practice, that of parish surgeon to a small village on the banks of the Clyde. Those in whose hands the appointment lay were not impressed with his fitness for the post, and he was not elected, "I felt," he afterwards said, "a deeper amount of chagrin and disappointment than I have ever experienced since that date. If chosen, I would probably have been working there as a village doctor still." Although such a commencement might have delayed his ultimate rise to eminence, it cannot be agreed that it could possibly have prevented it. It was at this crisis that what he tenderly referred to as "the ceaseless love and kindness of a dear elder brother" came to his rescue, and by Alexander's or, as he affectionately called him, "Sandy's" help, he returned to Edinburgh to resume his studies in the winter session, 1830-31. His other brother, David, had started in business as a baker at Stockbridge, close to Edinburgh, and James boarded with him there for a time. His qualification enabled him to become assistant to a Dr. Gairdner in dispensary practice, a class of work he had had some experience of in the previous year while staying with Dr. Girdwood at Falkirk during the summer. Dr. Gairdner was much struck with Simpson's abilities, which he

25

stated, "promised the most flattering expectations." In the course of his first experiences of actual practice he became impressed with the necessity for a knowledge of obstetrics, and therefore attended lectures on the subject by Dr. Thatcher, an extra-mural teacher of repute, who subsequently applied for the University chair of midwifery when Simpson was the successful candidate.

His chief object, however, was to qualify for the degree of Doctor of Medicine of the University, and this he succeeded in doing in 1832. The regulations for this coveted degree were, for the times, wonderfully complete; it was held in such high estimation and such large numbers qualified annually—in 1827 there were one hundred and sixty graduates—that the authorities felt justified in being stringent. The length of the course of study necessary for graduation had been fixed at four years, and required the candidate to have attended classes in Anatomy, Surgery, Materia Medica, and Pharmacy, the Theory and Practice of Medicine, Clinical Medicine, Midwifery, Chemistry, and Botany, as well as a three months' course in any two of the following:—Practical Anatomy, Natural History, Medical Jurisprudence, Clinical Surgery, and Military Surgery. The first step in examination took place at the house of one of the professors where the candidate was questioned in literary subjects, chiefly Latin, and in the different branches of Medicine and Surgery. If he passed this satisfactorily he was examined more minutely by two professors in the presence of the others, and was subsequently given two Aphorisms of Hippocrates to explain and illustrate in writing and to defend before the faculty, as well as two cases with questions attached. The last step was the presenting of a thesis which was read by one of the faculty and was publicly defended by the candidate on the day of graduation. All this examination was conducted in Latin. Simpson's thesis was entitled: *"De causa mortis in quibusdam inflammationibus proxima."* He was amongst the last graduates who were examined through the medium of Latin, for after 1833 the language was optional, and English soon became the only one used; at the same time the examinations were differently arranged, and made to consist of more thorough and prolonged written and oral stages. Being on a pathological subject, Simpson's thesis was allotted to Thomson, the professor of Pathology, to examine, who not only recommended the

26

author for the degree, but was so impressed by the ability displayed in the dissertation that he sought him out and promptly offered him the post of assistant, which Simpson as promptly accepted. This appointment was most welcome. Not only did it give him a much desired opportunity for pathological work, but the salary of £50 a year enabled him to free his family from the immediate necessity of supporting him.

If to MacArthur and John Reid was due the credit of first directing Simpson's thoughts to the study of medicine, to Professor John Thomson belongs the credit of having made him an obstetrician. "At Dr. Thomson's earnest suggestion and advice," says Simpson, "I first turned more especially to the study of midwifery with the view of becoming a teacher of this department of medical science." He lost no time in throwing himself heartily into the work that was nearest to him, and became almost indispensable to his chief. Most of his time was spent in the Pathological Museum, busily engaged in arranging, classifying, and describing the preparations, but he also assisted in preparing the professor's lectures. He took up more readily than Thomson the then new mode of study by the microscope, and it is related that once he composed a lecture for his chief on this subject which Thomson delivered without previous perusal. Several times as Thompson read the lecture to the class he looked up to glare at his assistant, and when they returned to the side room he shook his fist in his face, saying, "I don't believe one d—d word of it."

Although Simpson was now earning enough by his salary as assistant to meet his expenses at the time, his family maintained their loving interest in his welfare. His sister told him he was working too hard and hurting his health. "Well," he replied, "I am sure it is just to please you all."

Sandy, who had married in 1832, watched his career carefully, and when the cholera made its appearance in Scotland he made a will with a provision for "my dear James" in the event of his death. "I daresay," he addressed his family therein, "every one of you has a pleasure in doing him good by stealth as I have had myself."

By Thomson's advice Simpson attended Hamilton's lectures in the winter session 1833-4, and this time with awakened interest. With the definite object of devoting himself to Midwifery clearly in view Simpson worked with all his phenomenal energy during the years from 1832 to 1835, studying the subject while he was helping Thomson. He entered the front rank of the young graduates of his day, and was elected a member of the Royal Medical and Royal Physical Societies in the same year, 1833. Both these societies were for the encouragement of scientific study and discussion among students and young graduates, and to obtain the Presidential chair of either was a high honour. The Royal Medical Society was the oldest Society in the University, having been established in 1737 by the great Cullen and others; it had always been of great account in the University, and the originality of the utterances on professional matters which emanated from it made it then a power to be reckoned with not only in Edinburgh, but throughout European professional circles. For membership of the Royal Physical Society he was proposed by Edward Forbes, a brilliant youth, who subsequently distinguished himself in Natural History, and held the University Chair in that subject for a brief period until cut down prematurely at the age of thirty-nine. Forbes was the leader of a set of able young students who have left a distinct mark in the history of the University. John Reid was an intimate friend of Forbes, and Simpson was probably as intimate with him. Forbes was the founder and editor of the best of all the shortlived literary ventures of Edinburgh undergraduates—*The University Maga*, which was issued weekly in 1834; and he was also one of the founders of the Oineromathic Society, "The brotherhood of the friends of Truth." Forbes thus described the nature of this Society in song:—

"Some love to stray through lands far away,
Some love to roam on the sea,
But an antique cell and a college bell,
And a student's life for me.
For palace or cot, for mead or grot
I never would care or pine,
But spend my days in twining lays
To Learning, Love, and Wine."

"Wine, Love, and Learning" was the motto of this curious brotherhood, and it numbered in its membership many men of the day, who afterwards became eminent, such as Forbes himself, Reid, George Wilson, Goodsir, and Bennet. Simpson must have been quite cognisant of this Society's doings; he was closely associated with its leaders, but his name does not appear in any of the lists of members still preserved. His whole-hearted devotion to the ΜΑΘΗΣΙΣ probably prevented his uniting with the brotherhood to worship the ΕΡΩΣ and ΟΙΝΟΣ. The brotherhood was conspicuously united. In the great snowball riot of 1837, which was quelled only by the reading of the Riot Act and the marching down at the double from the Castle of the Cameron Highlanders into the University gates, they fought shoulder to shoulder.

In 1835 Simpson felt that the time had come to enter into serious practice and turn his acquired knowledge to account. Fifty pounds a year was no large income on which to satisfy his craving for learning, and there was no surplus from which by any means to repay his family for their assistance. Before taking any decided step, however, he desired to pay a visit to the Continental centres of medical science and teaching. The funds for the proposed tour were promptly found by his brothers Alexander and John; by their assistance he was enabled to visit Paris, Liége, and Brussels, as well as London and Oxford. He was accompanied by Dr. (now Sir Douglas) Maclagan, and kept a journal of the tour, which is an interesting example of his lively powers of observation. In London he visited the leading hospitals, and made the acquaintance of the leading physicians and surgeons, amongst whom were many *alumni* of his own *alma mater*. In the journal he freely and concisely criticised the men, their methods, and their hospitals. In Paris he followed the same plan, going the round of all the hospitals, and searching for and grasping the principle which guided each distinguished man's thought and teaching. He took more than a medical interest in all that he saw, and noted the appearance and habits of the people of each place that he visited. At the end of his coach ride from London to Southampton, on the way to Paris, he sat down to write:—"The ride as far as Windsor Park was delightful, and from the top of the coach we had two or three most lovely glimpses of English scenery. After passing Windsor the soil was rather inferior in many parts, and we passed every now and then large tracts of heath.... The neatness and cleanliness of the English cottages is greatly superior to all that we have in Scotland; the little patches of garden ground before, behind, and around them set them off amazingly. I wish the Scottish peasantry could by some means or other be excited to a little more love of cleanliness and horticulture. I did not see above two or three dirty windows, men or women along the whole line of road. The snow-white smock-frocks of the Hampshire peasantry do actually look well in my opinion."

At Liége on June 13th he wrote:—"And is it possible that I here begin a second volume of a journal?... I began my journal chiefly with some distant prospect of teaching myself the important lesson of daily notation. I am vain enough to flatter myself now that I have partly at least succeeded. At all events that which was at first a sort of task, at times rather an annoying task, has now become to me a pleasure. If I had my first volume to write over again I think I would now write it twenty times better. In writing a journal 'tis needless to think of making no blunders in the way of blots and bad grammar or of crooked sentences. We, or at least I, have occasionally felt so confoundedly tired at night that if I had been obliged to attend to such minutiæ I certainly would not have been able to advance above two sentences.

"This morning rose by half-past seven—dressed and breakfasted on coffee and rolls, read the *Liége Courier*, and by nine o'clock called on Professor Fohman with a copy of Dr. Reid's paper on the glands of the whale, which I had promised him yesterday. The Professor kept us until five minutes to ten, lecturing us on his discoveries upon the original elementary tubular structure of animal tissues. Somebody has remarked that no person ever entered into or at least came out of the study of the Book of Revelation without being either mad before or mad after it. I would not choose to say that Dr. F.'s case is perfectly analogous, but has it not some analogy? He seems to run wild on elementary tubular texture; ... he hates Lippi and his researches with a perfect hatred. Lippi has been preferred to him by the Parisian Academy. Is he not working against Lippi, and it may be against truth, if they happen to go together, which I do not believe?

"We have taken our seats in the diligence to-morrow for Louvain, and on leaving Liége I must confess that I leave one of the most lovely places I have seen on the Continent. 'Tis rich, populous, busy; the town in itself is old and good, though not so neat and clean as Mons; its environs wild and romantic. Besides it seems full of good-natured *gash* old wives, and sonsy, laughing-faced, good-looking, nay, some of them very good-looking girls."

The homeward journey was made *viâ* Birmingham, Liverpool, and Glasgow. In Liverpool he called upon a distant relative named Grindlay, established there as a shipper, and laid the foundation of a life-long friendship with the family. He also then for the first time met Miss Jessie Grindlay who afterwards became his wife.

With the end of this tour, Simpson brought to a close the more strictly student part of his career, although it remained true of him, as of all eminent scientific men, that he was a student to the end of his days. He felt himself now fully equipped to enter into the professional battle, and he stepped into the arena, not only full of vigorous life and hope, but possessed of highly trained faculties, keen senses, and lofty ideals. It was his strong, personal characteristics, apart from his accomplishments, which at once placed him head and shoulders above his fellows. "He had a great heart," says a recent writer, "and a marvellous personal influence, calling forth, not only the sympathy and love of his fellowmen, but capable of kindling enthusiasm in others almost at first sight." It is impossible to overestimate this personal influence in analysing the elements of his ultimate success, and it is more impossible for those who did not feel it to realise its nature; but that he became the beloved as well as the trusted physician is due to this influence. "He had no acquaintances," says the writer already quoted; "none could come into contact with him and stop short of friendship." This was a powerful trait to possess; it cannot be denied that he was fully aware of it and its value; and used it with good effect in establishing himself as the greatest physician of his day.

As a scientist he started with an eager desire for knowledge and reverence for truth, to which was added the highly developed power of mental concentration born of early self-training. When most men would be waiting in what they would term enforced idleness, Simpson would be busy with book or pen, deeply attentive to his occupation despite surrounding distractions or temptations to frivolous idleness. He took the full measure of the value of Time and handled his moments as another would a precious

31

metal. "At all times," he said himself, "on all occasions, and amidst the numerous disturbing influences to which the medical man is so constantly subjected, he should be able to control and command his undivided mental attention to the case or object that he may have before him.... In the power of concentrating and keeping concentrated all the energies of attention and thought upon any given subject, consists the power of thinking strongly and successfully upon that subject. The possession or the want of this quality of the mind constitutes the main distinction between the possession or the want of what the world designates 'mental abilities and talents.'"

His high ideals, his conception of the functions of the physician, and the strivings of the scientist are best shown in his own words:—"Other pursuits become insignificant in their objects when placed in contrast with ours. The agriculturist bestows all his professional care and study on the rearing of crops and cattle; the merchant spends his energies and attention on his goods and his commissions; the engineer upon his iron-wheels and rails; the sailor upon his ships and freights; the banker upon his bills and his bonds; and the manufacturer upon his spindles and their products. But what after all are machinery and merchandise, shares and stocks, consols and prices-current, or the rates of cargoes and cattle, of corns and cottons, in comparison with the inestimable value and importance of the very lives of these fellowmen who everywhere move and breath and speak and act around us? What are any, or what are all these objects when contrasted with the most precious and valued gift of God—human life? And what would not the greatest and most successful followers of such varied callings give out of their own professional stores for the restoration of health and for the prolongation of life—if the first were once lost to them, or if the other were merely menaced by the dreaded and blighting finger of disease?"

In one of his addresses of later years he urged upon his students the objects and motives which had been his in early professional life:—"The objects and powers of your art are alike great and elevated," he said. "Your aim is as far as possible to alleviate human suffering and lengthen out human existence. Your ambition is to gladden as well as to prolong the course of human life by warding off disease as the greatest of mortal evils; and restoring health, and even at times reason itself, as the greatest of mortal

32

blessings.... If you follow these, the noble objects of your profession, in a proper spirit of love and kindness to your race, the pure light of benevolence will shed around the path of your toils and labours the brightness and beauty that will ever cheer you onwards and keep your steps from being weary in well-doing; ... while if you practise the art that you profess with a cold-hearted view to its results, merely as a matter of lucre and trade, your course will be as dark and miserable as that low and grovelling love that dictates it."

Simpson's method of study was simple, at the same time that it involved immense labour. In entering upon a new work his first proceeding was to ascertain conscientiously all that had already been said or written by others upon the subject. He traced knowledge from its earliest sources and was able, as he followed the mental workings of those who had preceded him, to estimate the value of every vaunted addition to the sum of knowledge; and to weigh the theories and new opinions of men which had been evolved with the progress of time, and which had sometimes obscured, instead of casting greater light upon the truth. His antiquarian tastes added to his knowledge of Latin helped him in this work and turned a tedious task into a real pleasure. This preliminary accomplished, he plunged into the work of adding to the knowledge of the subject by thought, research, experiment, or invention.

In writing upon an abstract subject he would disentangle the confused thoughts of his predecessors and restate their opinions in direct and simplified language. But matters of opinion never had such an attraction for him as matters of fact; in dealing with these latter he would test by experiment the statements of authorities and correct or add to them by his own researches. Most of his professional writings, as well as his archæological works, are valuable for the historical *résumé* of the knowledge on the subject as well as for his additions. His later writings show as careful an attention to the inductive method with which he started, as those produced in the days of his more youthful enthusiasm; when fame was attained and fortune secured, when excessive work was sapping his physical strength, he never sank into lazy or slovenly methods in scientific work, but ever threw his whole vigour into the self-imposed task.

When studying Nature directly he was constantly asking her "why?"—just as in his notes of his teacher's lectures the query was ever recurring. He never felt himself beaten by an initial failure, but returned again and again with his questions with renewed energy each time. He was not to be denied, and in this manner he wrested from Nature some of those precious secrets the knowledge of which has relieved suffering and prolonged human life in every corner of the globe. "He never kept anything secret," says his nephew and successor, Professor A. R. Simpson, "that he thought could help his fellows, and it is hard to say whether his delight was greater in finding some new means to cure disease, or in demonstrating to others his methods of treatment."

He was indeed clothed in well-nigh impenetrable armour, and provided with powerful weapons, when in the autumn of 1835 he returned from his foreign tour to commence the serious fight in which his avowed object was not only to obtain professional eminence, but to stand forth a proud benefactor of the human race. Although he appealed always directly to Nature and used his own well-trained eyes and ears in preference to those of others, he did not completely brush aside authority as Sydenham had done; he hesitated neither to extract all that was valuable, nor to discard what appeared worthless from the writings of past masters.

CHAPTER IV

Early Practice and Professorship. 1835-1840

President of Royal Medical Society—Personal appearance—Practice among the poor—Corresponds with Miss Grindlay—Lecturer on obstetrics—Resignation of Professor Hamilton—Applies for vacancy—Active candidature—Strong opposition—Marriage—Account of the midwifery Chair—The medical professors at the time—Their opposition—Cost of candidature—Triumphant election.

In November, 1835, Simpson was elected one of the annual Presidents of the Royal Medical Society; a position which has been occupied by many young Edinburgh graduates, who have subsequently risen to fame. He took pains to make his inaugural address worthy of the occasion, and chose a subject connected with the pathology of obstetrics. It was a great success, and contributed largely towards giving him a recognised position as an authority in that branch of study. After appearing in the *Edinburgh Medical and Surgical Journal* for January, 1836, it was translated into French, Italian, and German. It also obtained for him his first foreign honour—one of a long list that was made up through his lifetime—that of corresponding member of the Ghent Medical Society; indeed, his early works received more attention and appreciation abroad than at home. In 1836, in order to widen his experience in his chosen subject, he filled the post of house-surgeon to the Lying-in Hospital, and held it for twelve months. He was also elected a Fellow of the Edinburgh College of Physicians. From this time he became a profuse writer on professional subjects, and developed an easy and convincing style; he carried on this work *pari passu* with practice amongst the poorer classes of the city and in addition to his work in connection with the Pathology Chair, always keeping in view his great object of becoming an obstetrician. It was not until 1838 that he became an independent lecturer on Midwifery. He had intended to do so earlier, but owing to Professor Thomson's ill-health, he had been called upon to act as Deputy-Professor of Pathology, a most valuable and useful employment.

35

Simpson's personal appearance at this time has been described by one who visited a meeting of the Royal Medical Society on an evening when he was in the chair:—"The chair was occupied," says the narrator, "by a young man whose appearance was striking and peculiar. As we entered the room his head was bent down, and little was seen but a mass of long tangled hair, partially concealing what appeared to be a head of very large size. He raised his head, and his countenance at once impressed us. A pale, rather flattish face, massive brent brows, from under which shone eyes now piercing as it were to your inmost soul, now melting into almost feminine tenderness; a coarsish nose with dilated nostrils, finely chiselled mouth which seemed the most expressive feature of the face ... Then his peculiar rounded soft body and limbs, as if he had retained the infantine form in adolescence, presented a *tout ensemble*, which even if we had never seen it again would have remained indelibly impressed on our memory."

In Simpson's youth physicians and surgeons made a habit of cultivating peculiarities of appearances and behaviour, but he was so shaped by nature as to attract attention without artificial aid. The growth of long hair seemed a natural accompaniment to his massive head and broad expressive countenance.

His practice at this time was scattered over the city, and he took long tramps in the course of the day. In one of his letters to his brothers, who were still loyally supporting him in his increasingly successful endeavours to establish himself after his heart's desire, he says:—"The patients are mostly poor it is true, but still they are patients; ... if my health is spared me, I do hope I may get into practice sufficient to keep me respectable after the lapse of years; but I know years must pass before that. At present I enjoy the best possible spirits and health, and with all my toils was never happier or healthier."

Tout vient à point à qui sait attendre. Simpson knew how to wait; he knew that waiting did not mean inactivity. Every opportunity that arose for advancement found him prepared to take full advantage of it.

That his lectures on pathology were acceptable was made manifest by the address presented to him by the students of the class at the end of his temporary term of office, testifying to his zeal, fidelity, and success, their admiration of his high talents, of the varied and extensive research which he displayed, and of his uniform and kind affability which, while it exalted him in the eyes of all as a teacher, endeared him to each as a friend.

During this period he kept up a correspondence with the Miss Grindlay, of Liverpool, whose appearance he had been struck with when he visited the family, and towards the end of 1837 he found time to visit there again accompanied by Dr. John Reid.

The way for his appearance as an extra-academical lecturer on midwifery was made clear at the end of 1837 by the death of Dr. Macintosh, a successful teacher of that subject. He had been in negotiation, without success, with this Dr. Macintosh for the taking over of the part or whole of his lectures, and found it easy to step at once into his place at his death. He was firmly determined to succeed ultimately to the University Chair of Midwifery. On one occasion he pointed out to some friends the then holder of the Chair, Professor Hamilton, thus:—"Do you see that old gentleman? Well, that's my gown!"

The good luck which had been his during his boyhood did not desert him when he began his course of lectures; for not only did he speedily attain a reputation for teaching, science, and practical skill, wonderful for one so young, but he had not two years to wait after thus establishing himself before the chair of his ambition fell vacant owing to the resignation in 1839 of Professor Hamilton, who died soon afterwards at the age of seventy-two.

It was a bold step for so young a man—for Simpson was only twenty-eight—to apply for the professorship. He was, however, not without his precedent. The second Monro obtained the Anatomy Chair at twenty-five, Alison filled that of Physic at thirty, and Thomas Hope and Alexander Christison were Professors of Chemistry and Medical Jurisprudence respectively each at the age of twenty-four. But this subject was one which was popularly thought to require a man of experience and especially a married man. Simpson had devoted his energies but partially to midwifery for only four or five years, and except for his short hospital appointment and recent experience as a lecturer on the subject had in the eyes of many no greater claim to the post than any other general practitioner, except in the fact that he had obtained a wide reputation in the science of the subject by his contribution to its literature and his researches. This last was the point on which he himself most relied; for his age he had done more scientifically than any of his opponents. Those who had watched his career knew that he possessed in addition to zeal and ability, brilliant teaching and practical powers. The objection of his youth was less easily got over than that of his unmarried state. With characteristic promptness, as soon as he had determined to apply for the Chair and found that as a bachelor his chances would be small, he disappeared for a time from Edinburgh, and returned triumphantly with Miss Jessie Grindlay, of Liverpool, as his wife. It was a bold stroke which delighted his supporters, discomfited his opponents, who saw therein the removal of a barrier to his success and a weapon from their hands, and astonished the worthy town councillors in whose gift the appointment lay.

The Edinburgh Chair of Midwifery was established in 1726, and was indisputably the first Chair of its kind in the British Islands, and probably in the world. It was in that year that the Town Council first established the medical faculty, by appointing two Professors of the Theory and Practice of Medicine and two of Medicine and Chemistry. A Chair of Anatomy had been instituted six years earlier through the instrumentality of the first Monro who became its first occupant. These five chairs were considered sufficient wherewith to teach all the medical knowledge of the day, and although appointed *ad vitam aut culpam* the professors received no remuneration out of the city revenues. The Chair was not reckoned at first as a faculty Chair, but was termed a city professorship. The newly created medical faculty would have no midwifery within the precincts of the University; and this is scarcely surprising when we remember that at first the only persons lectured to by the city professor were women of an inferior class in whose hands the practice of the art almost entirely lay.

Along with this appointment the Town Council established a system of regulation for midwifery practice within the city. It ordered that all midwives already in practice should at once be registered, and that no persons should thereafter enter on the practice within the city until they had presented to the magistrate a certificate under the hands of at least one doctor and one surgeon who were at the same time members of the College of Physicians or of the Incorporation of Chirurgeons, bearing that they had so much of the knowledge and principles of this art as warranted their entering on the practice of it; whereupon a licence should be given them signed by four magistrates at least entitling them to practise. It was further enacted that certain pains and penalties were to be inflicted upon ignorant persons for practising without this licence whereby their "want of skill might be of such dangerous consequences to the lives of so many people." It is to be presumed that as qualified medical men granted them these certificates and that these women had extensive practices, they possessed also a fair amount of skill. But slowly and gradually they had to give way and retire to the rank of nurses before the rise and growing public tolerance of the qualified male practitioner of obstetrics.

The second occupant of the chair, appointed in 1739, was elevated to a place in the medical faculty, but Professor Thomas Young, who occupied it in 1756, was the first to teach the subject to medical students by means of lectures and clinical instruction. As already noted, it was left for James Hamilton to obtain the recognition of midwifery as a subject, a knowledge of which was necessary for the obtaining of the University medical degree.

At the time when Simpson was straining every nerve to gain the post he coveted, the medical faculty of the University comprised the following professors of the following subjects:—Botany, Robert Graham, who established the Edinburgh and Glasgow Botanical Gardens; Anatomy, Monro the third; Chemistry, Hope, who discovered strontium in the lead mines of Argyleshire; Institutes of Medicine, Alison, an eminent physician and philanthropist who first pointed out the connection between destitution and epidemics of disease, and secured improved Poor Laws for his country; Practice of Physic, James Home; Materia Medica, Christison, the world-reputed toxicologist; Natural History, Robert Jameson; Clinical Surgery, James Syme, the wonderful operator and teacher, and inventor of the "macintosh" waterproof; Military Surgery, Ballingall; Medical Jurisprudence, Traill; Pathology, Thomson; and Surgery, Charles Bell, the discoverer of the double function of the nerves, who was ranked in his day on the Continent as greater than Harvey. It was thus not an undistinguished body that Simpson strove to enter; several of the best-known members were comparatively young men, recently appointed to their posts, and full of the rising scientific spirit. It is little to their credit that they were practically unanimous in opposing the candidature of this young and enthusiastic scientist, who afterwards shed such lustre on the University from the chair which they would have denied him for no reasons other than his youth and his humble origin.

Fortunately for Simpson and for the University, the appointment did not lie in the gift of the professors, but was entirely in the hands of the Town Council, comprising thirty-three citizens.

Such an election was always a matter of keen interest to the inhabitants of Edinburgh, and each candidate brought all the direct and indirect influence within his power to bear on every councillor whom he could reach. The Professors in the various faculties had no doubt great influence; they openly canvassed for the candidate they favoured, and did not hesitate to decry those they did not approve of. Shortsighted as this professorial opposition was, it proved no small difficulty in Simpson's way. Foremost amongst his opponents was Syme, who commenced a long feud with him by supporting his chief rival, Dr. Kennedy; "I feel no hesitation in stating," he wrote purposely for publication, "that of all the candidates in the field, he (Kennedy) is out of all question, according to my judgment, the one that ought to be elected." Sir Charles Bell was equally emphatic, and characterised Simpson's testimonials, in a note which Kennedy circulated, as given by "good-natured people merely to do a civil thing to a friend"—which was his mode of describing the declarations of some of the most eminent men of the day.

Each candidate also brought political influence to bear, and Whig and Tory grew agitated as the contest became keener. Simpson seems to have thought that both political parties were in opposition to him, but he certainly had the strong support of Ritchie of *Scotsman* fame, and the no less important influence of Mr. Duncan Maclaren.

When writing to ask Mr. Grindlay for his daughter's hand, Simpson candidly confessed his pecuniary position at the time. He referred to a debt of £200 already owing to his brother Sandy, and added:—"Again he gave me a bill for £120 to assist me in furnishing my house. This has been renewed and becomes due in January. He hopes to be able to pay it, and I fondly imagined I would have paid the half, but this canvass has involved me in new difficulties, and besides, I have endeavoured to assist my sister to go out to Van Diemen's Land. As it is now I am self-sufficient enough to think that I am as well off as regards station in my profession as any who started here in the race of life with me. They have all, I believe, been aided by friends or by private wealth. They have almost all been fortunate enough to have the protection of a father's roof during the first years of practice. I have had no such advantages, but have worked and stood alone. I have accumulated for myself a library and museum, worth £200 at least, amidst these difficulties. These I have won by my pen and my lancet, and these are my only fortune. And now could you trust her future happiness to me under such circumstances? I did not intend to ask her hand at present. I fondly hoped I might have *first* cleared myself of my debts."

Grindlay did not hesitate, but willingly gave his daughter, as she was willingly given, for better or worse.

The expenses of the canvass amounted to about £500, an amazingly large sum; he spared no expense in printing and posting his testimonials and letters to every one who had any influence with the Council, however small; but taking into consideration the cost of printing and postage in 1839, it is difficult to realise how the money was expended. His aim was to make known his scientific attainments, powers as a teacher, and personal qualifications which he felt, if duly realised, would outweigh the disadvantages of his youth and comparative inexperience. His testimonials spoke in strong terms of his abilities and characteristics; they were a good deal more numerous and elaborate than is customary to-day, but Kennedy's also made a fat volume of 150 octavo pages.

As the day of election drew near the excitement amongst citizens, professors, and students grew intense. Of the five candidates in the field, three, including his former teacher Thatcher, speedily fell out of the running. Dr. Evory Kennedy, of Dublin, and Simpson stood face to face as rivals. Kennedy was no mean opponent, and his supporters honestly considered him the better man of the two; his attainments certainly merited warm support. The prophets foretold a close struggle, and the event proved them

41

correct. So keen was public interest that when a report was circulated that Kennedy was a bad lecturer, his friends brought him over from Dublin a few days before the election, hired a public room, and made him lecture to a crowded and enthusiastic audience to dispel that illusion. In spite of this the popular vote was decidedly in Simpson's favour; if the citizens had had votes Simpson would have been returned at the head of the poll by a large majority.

On Tuesday, February 4, 1840, at a Council meeting, at which all thirty-three members were present, the Provost himself proposed Kennedy, while Baillie Ramsay proposed Simpson. The result was awaited with breathless suspense, the chamber being crowded by anxious spectators. Simpson's enthusiasm had infected his supporters; he had kindled the first sparks of that enthusiastic affection with which the citizens of Edinburgh ever after regarded him; when his triumph, by the narrowest majority, was announced, the cheers resounded loud and long.

The same evening he was able to write to Liverpool:—

"1, Dean Terrace.

"I was this day elected Professor. My opponent had sixteen and I had seventeen votes. All the political influence of both the leading Whigs and Tories here was employed against me; but never mind, I have got the chair in despite of them, Professors and all. Jessie's honeymoon and mine is to commence to-morrow."

It was the man's strong individuality which carried the day. The town councillors threw aside the political and academic bias of those who endeavoured to lead them, and elected the man who had boldly said, "Did I not feel I am the best man for the Chair I would not go in for it"; and had more boldly gone on showing them how thoroughly he felt what he said until they themselves came to believe it.

The gift of this Chair, as of many others in the University, has now passed from the hands of the Town Council into those of a body of curators, seven in number, three nominated by the University Court and four by the Town Council; such a body might have made a more cautious choice, but never a more fortunate one both for the city and the University than this of their long-headed and far-sighted predecessors.

CHAPTER V

Professor and Physician. 1840-1847

Success as a lecturer—Increased practice—Generosity—Fashionable patients—Memoir on Leprosy—Controversy concerning the Pathology Chair—Address to the Graduates, 1842—Squabbles—Purchases 52, Queen Street—A great and good physician—Called to London—Visit to Erskine House—The daily scene at 52, Queen Street—Rangoon petroleum and Christison—The disruption—His family—Appointed Physician-Accoucheur to the Queen for Scotland.

Simpson had not long been engaged upon his new duties before the town councillors gladly saw, and his brother professors were obliged to admit, that the baker's son was bringing a mighty genius to bear upon the subject of his choice from the chair of his ambition. He cherished no ill-feeling against those *confrères* who had actively opposed his candidature, but set to work amidst his new surroundings conscious that the best way to obliterate bitter feelings was by gradually creating a stronger feeling—that of respect for him as a man and a worker. He had dealt heavy blows himself during the conflict—blows not easily forgotten. The position demanded tact and patience, and he was not found wanting in either. He converted many who had worked against him into adherents, admirers, and even friends.

His lectures speedily attracted students. Besides those who were entering the profession, grey-headed and grey-bearded men, whose student days had long since passed away, came to sit at the feet of this remarkable young man and hear the so recently despised subject dealt with in his own masterly, scientific manner. Conciseness, clearness, and directness characterised his delivery; while with illustration and anecdote he made his dull subject fascinatingly interesting. It was his custom to write out on a black-board notes of the subject on which he was about to speak—concise, pithy headings, which were hung up in the theatre and which he proceeded methodically to explain and enlarge upon. So successful were his efforts that even in the first session he was able to make the proud boast that his class was for the first time in its history the largest in the University, and this in spite of the fact that one of the leading professors altered his lecture hour to the same hour as Simpson's, with the purpose of injuring the attendance at Simpson's class.

A direct result of the reputation obtained through his course of lectures and improved professional position was the rapid increase of his practice and the improvement of the class of his patients, so that pecuniary profit came within his reach. He continued to be a general practitioner, however, attending to all classes of cases that came to him; but his zeal for midwifery and the diseases of women, together with his renown in those subjects, brought mostly patients of the female sex to his consulting-room. With the improved position there came necessarily increased expenditure, which at first exceeded the income; he never stopped to consider the patients' circumstances or whether he was likely to be paid for his services. "I prefer to have my reward in the gratitude of my patients," he said. He treated all that came to him, and his generous nature was oftentimes taken advantage of by persons very well able to remunerate him; moreover, at this time, when his pecuniary profit did not equal his professional reputation, he cheerfully helped many who appealed to him with amounts he could ill spare.

His father-in-law generously and willingly stood by him until the fees began to come in more freely—his brother Sandy, who had supported him hitherto, having now other claims upon his purse. He found two ordinary but costly steps advisable—first, to move into a better and more centrally situated house; and, secondly, to obtain a carriage, "both to support my rank among my wealthier compeers and to save my body from excess of work." The outlay was justified in the result; the fees from students and from his private practice very soon enabled him to repay the debts to his brothers and his father-in-law without inconvenience and with grateful pleasure. Once and for ever within the first few years of his professorship he placed himself in a safe position, free from all pecuniary anxiety.

If he had laboured hard to fit himself for the front rank of his profession, his work on attaining that position showed increase rather than abatement. His private practice alone was the work of more than one ordinary individual, and his professorial duties took up some of the best hours of his day. In the evenings and at all odd times he busied himself with absorbing current or ancient literature, or in preparing his own contributions to both professional and general knowledge either with the pen or by experiment. "Oh that there were double twenty-four hours in the day," he sighed at a time when he was working at highest pressure, practising amongst peers, commoners, and cottagers alike, who all flocked to his residence or sent long distances for him. When Princess Marie of Baden, wife of the Duke of Hamilton, came under his special care in 1843 he felt that he was placed at the top of his profession in Scotland, and must have smilingly recalled the words of old Dr. Dawson, of Bathgate, when he heard of the successful contest for the Chair. "It's all very well," he had said, "to have got the Chair! But he can never have such a practice as Professor Hamilton. Why, ladies have been known to come from England to consult him!"

They came from the furthest parts of Greater Britain to consult Hamilton's successor, in spite of the old doctor's prognostication!

The energy as well as the versatility of the man is well shown in the works which he found time to carry on while he was thus establishing himself as a teacher and as a practitioner, during the years from 1840 to 1845. One of his first literary efforts, not wholly professional, the Memoir on "Leprosy and Leper-Houses," was produced at that time. It was a work of relaxation and pleasure, for it carried him deeply into his favourite archæology. The fascination which this subject always had for him sprang from his love of nature, and of the greatest work of nature—man. "The leading object and intent of all the antiquarian's pursuit is MAN," he said, "and man's ways and works, his habits and thoughts, from the earliest dates at which we can find his traces and tracks upon the earth, onwards and forwards along the journey of past time. During this long journey he has everywhere left scattered behind him and around him innumerable relics forming so many permanent impressions and evidences of his march and progress."

The quantity and quality of the information concerning leper hospitals which he collected and embodied in his memoir, contributed to the Edinburgh Medico-Chirurgical Society in March, 1841, was phenomenal. He had consulted old manuscripts and registers, monastic chronicles, burgh records, and Acts of Parliament, as well as works of antiquity, travel, and history. He gave close upon five hundred references, as well as a list of one hundred and nineteen leper-houses, whose existence in Britain and whose history he had traced. The work illustrates the objects and proper methods of antiquarian research, which twenty years afterwards he dilated upon in his address from the Chair of the Scottish Society of Antiquaries. In the course of it he pointed out how vigorously our ancestors had set to work to stamp out the disease when it spread through Europe during the period from the tenth to the sixteenth century. The method adopted was that still employed—segregation; about the twelfth century scarcely a town or burgh in France and Britain was without its leper-hospital. Although we in Britain are happily now freed from its ravages, other parts of the world are not so fortunate. It is still regarded popularly as an incurable disease, as it was in 1597, when one Catherine Livingstone was gravely brought to trial for witchcraft, one instance of which had been that she dared to state her ability to cure "leprosie, which the maist expert men in medicine are not abil to do." The indictment set forth that she "took a reid cock, slew it, baked a bannock with the blude of it, and gaf the samyn to the leper to eat." The witch's remedy is scarcely more curious and certainly no less useful than those recommended two centuries later by John Wesley in his "Primitive Physic," where, moreover, he cheerfully, if somewhat too briefly to satisfy the modern inquirer, reports the cure "of a most desperate case" by the drinking of a half-pint of celery-whey morning and evening.

Scotland was severely smitten by leprosy in the centuries when it overspread Europe; Robert Bruce fell a victim to it in 1339, and the disease seems to have lingered in the North after it had almost vanished from England.

Simpson's paper was published in the *Edinburgh Medical and Surgical Journal* in three parts in 1841 and 1842, and to this day is the most valuable contribution to the interesting and important history of the disease. Some of the information had been collected in his student days. In his antiquarian researches he had frequently met with references to the dirty and unwholesome habits and surroundings of Scots towns in early days. The thought that dirt and disease were directly connected—a new thought even so recently as fifty years ago—led to his investigations. He found that leprosy was most prevalent at the time when his country was most dirty; but he was not able to establish his supposition that the cause of the disease lay in the insanitary surroundings of the people; indeed his researches proved that, on the contrary, leprosy had declined and practically disappeared from the country long before any material improvement in sanitary conditions took place.

Simpson's conduct when Professor Thomson resigned the Chair of Pathology illustrates the vigour with which he entered into quite casually arising incidents where he saw that strength and a fight were necessary to conquer an evil or prevent an abuse. Thomson resigned in 1841 owing to ill-health. The Chair had been established by William IV. in 1831 on the representations of Thomson himself, who succeeded in satisfying Lord Melbourne that the subject was worthy of the dignity of a separate Chair, in spite of the protests of the Senatus Academicus, who throughout the history of the medical faculty generally appear to have been actuated more by personal considerations and professional jealousies, where new developments were in process, than by zeal for their *Alma Mater*. Professors Syme and Alison actively led an agitation that with Thomson's resignation the separate teaching of pathology should be brought to an end. Without a moment's hesitation, in the midst of his hard work, and suffering from indifferent health, Simpson plunged into a controversy with these colleagues, in which he silenced at once and for ever the detractors who had sneered at him as an ignorant, uncultured man-midwife. The controversy as usual was followed with intense interest by Edinburgh folks, and Simpson received a first taste of that popular approval which undoubtedly was one of the enjoyments of his life. The Crown avoided the difficulty of deciding between the rival petitioners for and against the Chair by transferring its patronage to the Town Council, who showed the same foresight which had led them to appoint Simpson, in deciding to maintain its existence. Unfortunately their wisdom failed when they elected as Thomson's successor a man who, although of brilliant attainments, subsequently brought discredit upon his University and himself by becoming a convert to homœopathy. Simpson, who was indirectly instrumental in securing the Chair of Pathology for this man became his bitterest opponent when he declared himself a follower of

48

Hahnemann's unorthodox and mistaken doctrines.

In 1842 it fell to Simpson's lot to deliver the customary address to the medical graduates after they had received their degrees at the annual ceremonial on the 1st of August. He treated his listeners to a discourse on the duties of young physicians. When we remember that he had attained to his then high professional position while he was no more than a young physician himself, we recognise that he was but setting forth the ideals and principles which had been and still were his guides in life and conduct.

After warning his audience against regarding the gaining of the coveted degree as the end of their student career, instead of as in reality the opening up of a lifetime of observation and study, he pointed out that self-patronage was the best of all patronage. "Place from the first," he said, "all your hopes of advancement upon the breadth and extent of your medical abilities alone.... Rather walk by the steady light of your own lamp than by the more dazzling, but to you more uncertain, lustre borrowed from that of others ... Young physicians often dream that by extending the circle of their private acquaintances they thus afford themselves the best chance of extending the circle of their private patients.... No man will in any case of doubt and danger entrust to your professional care the guardianship of his own life or of the life of those who are near and dear to his heart, merely because you happen to be on terms of intimacy with him. The self-interest of human nature forbids it.... The accomplishments which render you acceptable in the drawing-room are not always those that would make your visits longed for or valued in the chamber of sickness and sorrow.... Give therefore your whole energies to medicine; and in its multiplied departments you will find 'ample room and verge enough' for the most energetic as well as the most comprehensive mind. Place your faith in no extrinsic influences. Let your own professional character be the one great patron to whom you ever look for your professional advancement." He exhorted the young practitioners above all to save and economise their time, and to regard it as a property to be avaricious of and of every item of which they were to render a proper account to themselves. "It is by carefully preserving, confirming, and making diligent use of these broken and disjointed portions of it, which others thoughtlessly waste and destroy, that almost all the highest reputations in the medical profession have been formed." He strongly urged the value of a "proper covetousness of time." "Look around, and you will find that those who have the most to do in the way of business as practitioners have also apparently the most time to spare as observers and writers.... And why? Because they have all their daily duties perfectly assorted and arrayed; they save from loss and destruction every possible fragment of time and this very industry and precision procures them more true leisure than indolence can boast of."

In referring to the relation of practitioner to patient, he spoke on a subject which has been much discussed in recent years without altering the principle originally laid down in the oath of Hippocrates:—"Whatever," said Simpson, "is communicated to you as a matter of professional confidence, must ever remain buried within your own breasts in all the silence and secrecy of the grave." He concluded his address with well-judged remarks on the relation of the physician to his professional brethren, counselling his hearers to observe the Golden Rule, and, moreover, "if it be possible, as much as lieth in you, live peaceably with all men; never allow the darker part of your nature to persuade you to the attempt of over-taking him who has distanced you in the race of life by any unjust efforts to lame the character, and thus diminish the speed, of your adversary. And if such attempts are made upon you by others, have no dread of them—if you are armed strong in honesty, if you have pursued a line of irreproachable truth and unbending rectitude of conduct. 'Be thou as pure as snow thou shalt not escape calumny.'... Your future career is a matter of your own selection, and will be regulated by the conduct which you choose to follow. That career may be one of happiness or self-regret, one of honour or of obscurity, one of wealth or of poverty. The one or other result is not a matter of *chance*, but a matter of choice on your part. Your diligence and industry for the next few years will almost inevitably secure for you the one; your apathy and indolence will almost inevitably entail upon you the other. May God, in His infinite goodness, enable you to select the wiser and the better path."

In this address, as in that previously quoted, we hear him exhorting his young listeners to a line of conduct which we know to have been broadly his own in practice as well as in ideal. During these early years as professor,

Simpson had to ward off many ill-disposed adversaries, and he met their attack with the determination and powerful preparedness that characterised his attitude in later years, when he experienced the hostility so constantly opposed to genuine reformers, and men who have lived ahead of their times. He sometimes regarded these encounters regretfully himself; but none the less remembered to

"Bear't that the opposed may beware."

The correspondence pertaining to some of these disputes was filed and ticketed, with brief contempt, "Squabbles." His controversy with Professor Syme over a personal matter in 1845 was not to the credit of either of these great men, and, as Simpson himself confessed, was equally discreditable to their profession. Simpson had seen, as has been pointed out, several of his teachers fighting long and strongly for their own cherished objects; and he doubtless then, in his student days, learnt the lesson that vigorous persistence had the power to gain much that at first seemed hopeless; he fought with such energy, that he accomplished in his own lifetime what the example of others might have led him to think would have been accomplished only by his successors.

The growth of his practice up to 1847 was little short of phenomenal. In 1845 he purchased No. 52, Queen-street, the house which he inhabited up to his death, and which became the Mecca of hundreds upon hundreds of pilgrims from all quarters of the globe. Here, in those years, he was sought and consulted by unceasing crowds; in the public mind he was undoubtedly endowed with more than human powers, and regarded as a magician, at the wave of whose wand pain and disease would vanish. This caused him much embarrassment, and brought upon him the abuse of ignorant persons, irritated to find that, after all, even in Simpson's person, there was a limit to human powers; or of others with unimportant ailments who were disappointed to find that, once having made his diagnosis of their condition, he would have no more of them, preferring to place his time at the disposal of those whose sufferings were real and capable of relief, or whose cases were complicated and interesting. The question of remuneration was always secondary, and so careless was he in pecuniary matters that it is related that he would wrap up interesting specimens, professional or antiquarian, in bank notes; and his trusted valet was in the habit of emptying his pockets at night of the money earned in the day, to prevent its being lost, mislaid, or given away to undeserving persons. With him work was first and fee second. Like a great modern teacher he was able to say, "Work first—you are God's servant; fee first—you are the fiend's." To Simpson "work was master and the Lord of Work, who is God."

The personal power and attractiveness of the man were large factors in gaining the practice which he now enjoyed. But he did not depend for success on these alone, by any means. His professional reputation was fully won by great work in obstetrics and gynæcology, and by the introduction of methods and instruments which contributed to the saving of countless lives. It has been said that he gave a new life to the obstetric art, and presided at the birth of gynæcology. He had done this before the great deed was dreamt of which hands his name down to posterity, before his discovery of the anæsthetic power of chloroform. Simpson was a great physician, the leading practitioner of the art and exponent of the science with which his name will always be connected. But many great physicians have failed to fulfil as Simpson did, Robert Louis Stevenson's description of the physician:—

"Generosity he has such as is possible to those who practise an art, never to those who drive a trade; discretion tested by a hundred secrets; tact tried in a thousand embarrassments; and what are more Heraclean cheerfulness and courage. So it is that he brings air and cheer into the sick room, and often enough, though not so often as he wishes, brings healing."

Great as a man and great as a physician, Simpson was actually run after by the greatest in the land. In 1845 he was summoned professionally to London, and gave an interesting description of his kindly reception by the Duchess of Sutherland and her family in a letter written from Stafford House. His advent to London was a matter of notoriety, and he noted that he bought in the street a life of himself which mightily diverted him and made him laugh until he was sore. A year or more later he was invited for rest and change to Erskine House by Lord Blantyre, where he says, "the Duchess of Sutherland, the Marquis and Marchioness of Lorne, and two Ladies Gower have made up with myself all the strangers." "Tell Janet," he wrote to his brother, "I think now artificial flowers very ungenteel. The ladies here wear nothing but real flowers in their hair, and every day they come down with something new and for us males to guess at. Often the Duchess wears a simple chaplet of ivy leaves, sometimes a bracken leaf is all she sports in her head ornaments, and beautiful it looks. Rowans and 'haws' are often worn beaded into crowns or flowers or chaplets. Heather is also a favourite. On Thursday Lady Lorne came down with a most beautiful chaplet tying round and keeping down her braided hair. It was a long bunch of bramble leaves and half-ripe bramble berries—actual true brambles. They have been all exceedingly kind to me, and I really feel quite at home among them though the only untitled personage at table."

The daily scene at 52, Queen Street was now unique. Those who had the fortune to lunch or breakfast in that hospitable house never forgot it. Statesmen, noblemen, artists, scientists, clergymen, and politicians from various countries sat down together and entertained each other or attempted to do so in their different languages. The host guided the conversation while he still glanced over the newspaper or some newly published book, and never failed by skilful leading to entice out of every one the best knowledge that they possessed. With his quick insight he rarely failed in his estimate of character, but rapidly perceived even in a stranger where the conventional ceased and the real man began.

No stranger to Edinburgh omitted to bring or obtain an introduction to the genial professor; all were welcome, and an open table was kept. The scene has been described from intimate knowledge in the columns of the *Scots Observer* as follows:—"Luncheon is set on the table, and some ten, twenty, or even fifty people wait the appearance of their host, who is on his rounds maybe, or in another room ministers to an urgent case. A stranger who has not learnt that the great Simpson was only in the broadest sense a punctual man—of minutes, hours, he knew nothing, but none more reliably punctual, few so unsparingly regular in working while 'tis called to-day—might be prompted by hungry discontent to suggest that none but the wealthiest can keep the doctor from his guests. The mere suggestion would be infamous, for rich and ragged alike pay fees or not exactly as it pleases them. Whatever the cause, the host still lingers, and the impatient stranger has time to wonder how it is that so odd an assortment of human beings should be met together in one room. Lords and Commons rub shoulders at his table; the salt of the earth sit down side by side with the savourless; tweed jostles broadcloth; the town-bred Briton looks askance at his country-bred compatriot, and both unconsciously shudder at the Briton with no breeding at all. In one room are assembled together the American of bluest blood; the Yankee bagman; the slave-owning Southerner, and even the man of colour hateful to both alike. The atmosphere is chill like the grave, each guest, eyeing his neighbour suspiciously, shrinks into his own social shell; on each face the meanness and snobbery of humankind is, if not aggressively expressed, at least clearly legible; when all at once Simpson bustles in. In a few minutes, under the genial influence of his presence, all tongues are set a-wagging, and well may you ask whether the men who leave his house after luncheon are those who half-an-hour ago regarded each other with cold disdain. For now they are cordial, kindly, sympathetic; each has been induced to show whatever was attractive in his nature, or to give the fruits of his experience. If in one short hour Simpson could thus transform a crowd of frigid, haughty strangers into an assemblage of decent, amiable human beings, what could he not achieve in a day, a year, or a life?"

His reception of members of his own profession was specially cordial, and if those from any one country were more welcome than others, it was the many who crossed the Atlantic to see and hear him. America had the greatest share in the birth of anæsthetics, and Simpson's intimacy with so many of the profession in the United States made it easy for them to welcome his assistance in that great event. Gynæcology, too, was eagerly taken up in America, and many were Simpson's admirers from that country who returned home fired by his influence to work out for themselves valuable additions to that science.

Simpson paid close attention to current events in other branches of science, in politics, and in religion. Sir Robert Christison and he were at one time associated in an enterprise which narrowly escaped being the source of a fortune to him. Rangoon petroleum which was obtained from pits dug on the banks of the Irawaddy had been chemically investigated by Christison, and he had isolated from it a substance which he named petroline; unfortunately, unknown to him, a German chemist had independently made the same discovery a few months earlier, and christened the substance paraffin. When, a few years later, it occurred to Simpson that the crude Rangoon petroleum might serve as a lubricant for machinery and prove cheaper than those in general use, he applied to Christison. He met with willing assistance, but a refusal on principle to have anything to do with a patent, which Christison laughingly suggested, might be called "Simpson's incomparable antifriction lubricant!"

"When I called for Simpson," says Christison, in his Recollections, "his two reception rooms were as usual full of patients, more were seated in the lobby, female faces stared from all the windows in vacant expectancy, and a lady was ringing the door bell. But the doctor brushed through the crowd to join me, and left them all kicking their heels for the next two hours."

Their experiments proved that petroleum was vastly superior to sperm oil, the best known and most commonly used lubricant. Simpson proceeded to take out a patent, having no such scruples as Christison; but to his chagrin found that he had been forestalled by others, and had to abandon the subject.

About the period now referred to Scotland was stirred from end to end by the ecclesiastical movement which culminated in the crisis known as the Disruption, when, for reasons connected with the jurisdiction of the National Church, a majority of its members severed their connection therewith in a public and dramatic fashion, and "came out" to found the now strong and vigorous Free Kirk. Simpson at first steered clear of all the squabbles and discussions which the movement gave rise to, but when affairs approached a crisis he threw his lot in with the leaders of the new movement, and became a staunch Free Churchman.

Busy as he was, Simpson fully enjoyed his home and all the inner domestic life. He was a cheery and hearty host to his intimate friends, and took a pleasure in impromptu entertainments got up by himself in his own house, when he found time at his disposal for such amusement. His first child—a daughter—of whom he was mightily proud, was born in 1840; his first son, David, in 1842; and the second, Walter, in 1843. In 1844 the young couple, in the midst of their rising prosperity, suffered the loss of their daughter, who died after a brief illness. Simpson felt the loss keenly, and wrote pathetically on the subject to his relations; long afterwards he loved to talk of her and her winning ways.

By 1846 the vast majority of his work lay in obstetrics and gynæcology, although he himself would no doubt have indignantly repelled the suggestion that he was a specialist; his mind recognised the interdependence of all the great branches of the healing art, and the necessity for any who wished to excel or be useful practitioners to be *au courant* with each and every branch. He had early shown that as a pathologist alone he was worthy of a niche in the temple of fame; and in later days he was urged to apply for the vacant chair of Physic in his own University; while Professor A. R. Simpson tells us that foreigners working in the sphere of surgery sometimes spoke of him as a surgeon.

Early in 1847 his good friend, the Duchess of Sutherland, wrote to inform him that the Queen had much pleasure in conferring upon him the vacant post of Physician to Her Majesty. In the Queen's own words, "His high character and abilities made him very fit for the post." He held this post until his death, under the title of Physician Accoucheur to the Queen for Scotland.

Thus in his thirty-sixth year, to the pride of his family and of the whole village community in which he had been born and received his early training, to the admiration of patients and friends, as well as to his own conscious satisfaction, the Bathgate baker's son had risen by his own efforts to the highest attainable position in his native land. But the work which was to make him one of the most conspicuous figures in the history of medicine, and raise him to a place of honour in the grateful estimation of humanity, was scarcely begun.

CHAPTER VI

The Discovery of Anæsthetics. 1844-1847

His early sympathy for suffering—Surgical methods before the discovery of anæsthetics—His mental struggle caused by the sickening sights of the operating theatre—His researches into the history of anæsthesia—Indian hemp—Mandrake—Alcohol—Hypnotism and other methods—Inhalation of drugs—Sir Humphry Davy—Anæsthetics discovered in America—Horace Wells and laughing-gas—Morton and ether—Ether in Great Britain—He uses it in midwifery practice—Search for a better-anæsthetic—Discovery of anæsthetic power of chloroform.

From his earliest student days the desire had ever been present in Simpson's mind to see some means devised for preventing the sufferings endured by patients on the operating table, without, as he put it, "interfering with the free and healthy play of the natural functions." It is difficult for us at the close of the nineteenth century to understand, without an effort of the imagination, the strong incentives which he had for such a wish. Even to-day, when operations are conducted without the infliction of pain, young students are not unfrequently overcome by the sight and the thought of what is in front of them. At the commencement of a winter session the theatre is crowded with those students who are entering upon surgical study, and with others, not so far advanced, who have come to get a preliminary peep at the practice of this fascinatingly interesting art. Many of these at first succumb and faint even before the surgeon has begun his work, and sometimes are only persuaded to pursue their studies by the encouragement of kindly teachers.

Simpson also went through this trying experience, but it must have been a greater struggle to him to persist. The surroundings of the surgeon at the commencement of the century were vastly more repugnant to a youth of sensitive nature than to-day. The operating theatre then has been compared to a butcher's shambles; cleanliness was not considered necessary, and little attention was paid to the feelings of the patient. He was held down by three or four pairs of powerful arms as the surgeon boldly and rapidly did his work, despite the screams, stopping, perhaps, only to roughly abuse the patient for some agonised movement which had interfered with the course of action. The poor wretch saw the instruments handed one by one by the assistant, and heard the surgeon's calm directions and his remarks on the case. The barbarous practice of arresting bleeding by the application of red-hot irons to the surface of the wound had indeed ceased three centuries before, when that humane reformer, Paré, displaced it with the method of tying the open blood-vessel, but the patient's blood gushed forth before him until arrested, into the sawdust spread to receive it, and the sight and the hot odour of it oftentimes mercifully caused him to faint. The spirit of Paré who, when relating a successful operation, would humbly add at the end, "I dressed him; God healed him," had not descended to those who practised in Simpson's day the art for which Paré did so much. It had grown to be necessary for a surgeon to be rough and callous; it was expected of him by the public; he was a man to be pointed at in the street, and shuddered at when he passed, by all who devoutly prayed they might escape his clutches. Much of this conduct was mere mannerism; it had become the custom, and had to be maintained in order to preserve the dignity and stamp the identity of the surgeon. Much of it arose from the haste with which the surgeon had to work; the quicker the operation the better chance had the patient; it was no uncommon thing to see a bystander timing the surgeon's work, as the professional time-keeper carefully times a race; and the rapidity of each surgeon's performances was a subject of comparison and admiration amongst the students of his day. Much of it also arose from the effect of the hideous scenes in the operating room upon the surgeon himself; his nerve had to become of iron if he desired to succeed, and with the nerve the face and the manner, but not necessarily always the heart hardened also. Tennyson possibly recollected these days, when he wrote of the surgeon who

> "Sent a chill to my heart when I saw him come in at the door,
> Fresh from the surgery schools of France, and of other lands;
> Harsh red hair, big voice, big chest, big merciless hands."

When Simpson first saw Liston raise his knife to operate on a poor

58

Highland woman, he actually felt so repelled that he contemplated abandoning his studies, and made a serious attempt to enter upon legal work instead. But the mental struggle with which medical men of all countries, and in all times, can sympathise out of their own knowledge, ended in a victory for medicine, and a triumphant return to his studies with the question permanently engraved on the tablets of his mind, "Can nothing be done to prevent this suffering?"

It is necessary and it is certainly beneficial that we should thus remind ourselves of the horrors which surrounded the surgeon so recently as sixty years ago. "Before the days of anæsthetics," wrote an old patient to Simpson, in a letter which he treasured with pride—the writer was himself a medical man—"a patient preparing for an operation was like a condemned criminal preparing for execution. He counted the days till the appointed day came. He counted the hours of that day till the appointed hour came. He listened for the echo in the street of the surgeon's carriage. He watched for his pull at the door bell; for his foot on the stair; for his step in the room; for the production of his dreaded instruments; for his few grave words, and his last preparations before beginning. And then he surrendered his liberty and, revolting at the necessity, submitted to be held or bound, and helplessly gave himself up to the cruel knife.".

It was, indeed, a monstrous ogre this giant Pain, holding the poor weak human creature in its merciless clutches, which Simpson even in his youthful days bethought himself to attack. It is well that we who are the heirs, should know how Simpson and those others whose names are ever associated with his, slew the monster, won the victory, and championed the human race forward into a land where further victories undreamt of by themselves are now being daily won.

Simpson searched into ancient history in order to ascertain the methods, if any, by which in remote and mediæval times surgeons sought to prevent the pain of operations. The most time-honoured method seems to have been by the internal administration of drugs, the chief one used being Indian hemp, which was well known in the East, and under one of its names *haschish* gave origin to the term assassin (strictly eater of haschish). A certain Arab Sheikh got together a band of followers to whom he administered haschish, which produced in them its usual effect—beautiful dreams of a delightful paradise. He induced them to believe so thoroughly in his power to gain for them at death permanent entrance to this paradise that they obeyed all his ferocious and bloodthirsty behests. Thus these assassins became known as men obedient to their leader in any murderous enterprise. Indian hemp was, and still is, used as a luxury all over the East, as well as to annul pain, and was used by criminals doomed to torture or execution. Simpson thought the *nepenthe* of Homer was a preparation of this drug; he also refers to the fact that Herodotus relates that the Massagetæ inhaled the vapour of burning hemp to produce intoxication and pleasurable excitement.

Mandrake was used in a similar manner and for similar purposes as Indian hemp in the Middle Ages, but it fell into disuse on account of the fatal results that often followed. It is frequently referred to by Shakspeare both for its narcotic properties and for its fabulous power of uttering a scream when torn up by the roots, to hear which meant death or madness. Simpson cited also well-known passages from Shakspeare to prove that the practice of "locking up the spirits a time" was known to that poet.

In later days the intoxication produced by alcohol was taken advantage of, and instances of its use have been known in quite recent years in the Colonies, where both a surgeon and chloroform were out of reach.

No drug, however, was known to be of such value in producing anæsthesia as to be constantly used, and many trials were made of other means, notably that of compressing the nerves supplying the part to be operated upon, but this was found to be too painful in itself. The stupor produced by compressing the carotid arteries—a method taken advantage of by the ruffians known as garotters—was also put in practice for a time during the sixteenth and seventeenth centuries, but it was found too barbarous a method even for those days.

Hypnotism was known to the Indians, Egyptians, and Persians at a very remote period, and may possibly have been used by them sometimes to produce anæsthesia for surgical purposes. Simpson was attracted by the words of the poet Middleton in his tragedy "Women, beware Women" (1617) where he says—

"I'll imitate the pities of old surgeons

To this lost limb—who ere they show their art
Cast me asleep, then cut the diseased part."

When hypnotism made one of its periodic re-appearances in 1837, this time under the name of mesmerism, after that extraordinary exponent of its powers Mesmer, Simpson recognised in it a possible method for "casting the patient asleep" before operation and set to work to investigate its phenomena. A Frenchman named Du Potet, disheartened by the prejudice against mesmerism in his own country, came to London in 1837, and was fortunate enough to receive the support of Dr. John Elliotson, physician to University College Hospital. Elliotson's advocacy of the new practice was received with ridicule by the profession, and was treated with such scathing contempt by the *Lancet* and other journals, that he was completely ruined.

Simpson was very successful in his experiments with mesmerism, conducted on the lines suggested by Elliotson, but he recognised that, after all, it was not the agent for which he was seeking, and dropped his researches.

He did not resume them even when Liston, a few years later, stimulated by the advocacy of the Manchester surgeon Braid, who met with a better reception than Elliotson, and by the relation of a long series of successful cases by a surgeon named Esdaile, in Calcutta, actually performed operations with success on patients brought under its influence.

The first suggestion to produce anæsthesia by the *inhalation* of drugs was made by Sir Humphry Davy in 1800. He discovered by experiment upon himself that the inhalation of *nitrous oxide* gas—commonly known as a *laughing gas*—had the power of relieving toothache and other pains; he described the effect as that of "uneasiness being swallowed up for a few minutes by pleasures." Although he stopped short at this stage, and does not seem to have used the inhalation to produce actual loss of consciousness, he, nevertheless, forecast the future by suggesting that nitrous oxide might be used as an inhalation in the performance of surgical operations, in which "no great effusion of blood" took place.

Some thirty years later Faraday pointed out that *ether* had effects upon the nervous system when inhaled, similar to those of laughing-gas. These two drugs came to be inhaled more in jest than in earnest; more as an amusing scientific experiment for the sake of the pleasure-giving excitement they set up, than for the purpose Davy had suggested. Ether, it is true, was recommended even before Davy's day for the relief of the suffering in asthma, but until the fifth decade of the century no one had attempted to prevent suffering as inflicted by the surgeon or the dentist, by producing the state of unconsciousness brought about by the inhalation of such drugs as ether—a process now known to the world as anæsthesia.

The persons who first made the bold experiments which resulted in the discovery of how to produce anæsthesia were Americans; and two men were prominently concerned in the discovery. Several others made isolated and successful efforts with both ether and nitrous oxide, but they lacked the confidence and the courage to make their success public and to persist in their experiments. Of these, Dr. Long, of Athens, Georgia, was one of the earliest; he is said to have successfully removed a tumour from a patient under the influence of ether in 1842, and in the Southern States he is regarded as the discoverer of anæsthesia. Dr. Jackson, of Boston—a scientific chemist—laid claim to the honour of the discovery after others had fought the fight and established the practice of anæsthesia. Neither of these men, for the reason already given, deserves the honour which is now universally attributed to their fellow-countrymen, Wells and Morton.

Horace Wells was born at Hartford, Connecticut, in 1815, and was educated to the profession of dental surgeon. He gave much attention to the desire present in the minds of many men at that time to render dental operations painless. On December 10, 1844, he witnessed at a popular lecture the experiment of administering laughing-gas, and noticed that a Mr. Cooley, while still under the influence of the gas, struck and injured his limb against a bench without suffering pain. The idea at once occurred to Wells that here was the agent he was in search of, and the very next day he experimented upon himself. If it has ever been fortunate to have toothache it was so for Wells that day; he was troubled by an aching molar which was removed by a colleague named Rigg, whilst he was fully under the influence of nitrous oxide; and thus he began what he himself at once called on recovering consciousness, "a new era in tooth-pulling." He proceeded promptly to test the experiment upon others and with complete success; and then making his success known, he proceeded with his former pupil Morton to Boston, and gave a public demonstration of his method which unfortunately was so imperfectly carried out that he was laughed at for his pains and stigmatised an impostor. Wells himself stated that the failure was due to the premature withdrawal of the bag containing the gas, so that the patient was but partially under its influence when the tooth was extracted. Wells and Morton were ignominiously hissed by the crowd of practitioners and students gathered to see the operation. Wells never recovered from the disappointment and the illness which resulted, and although he was able to explain his discovery to the French Academy of Science in 1846, he unfortunately died insane in New York two years later. Undoubtedly he was the first to discover the practicability of nitrous oxide anæsthesia, and to proclaim the discovery with a discoverer's zeal. Although his career ended so sadly, his efforts had, nevertheless, inspired to greater endeavour his colleague Morton, who had not only been associated in his experiments, but had been deeply interested in the subject for many years.

William Thomas Green Morton was born in 1819; his father was a farmer at Charlton, Massachusetts. He qualified as a dentist at Baltimore, and entered into successful practice at Boston. Fired with the same ambition as Wells, he made attempts to extract teeth painlessly with the assistance of drugs administered, or sometimes of hypnotism. In December, 1844, after Wells's failure with nitrous oxide gas, he wisely abandoned that agent and investigated another which promised better results. He experimented first with a drug known as *chloric ether*, but failing to get the desired effect, and at the suggestion of the aforementioned Dr. Jackson, he proceeded to investigate the effect of ordinary ether. The first experiments were made on animals, and were so encouraging that he believed he had at last found the desired agent, provided the effect on human beings corresponded with that upon dumb creatures. Boldly and heroically he made the necessary experiment upon himself, and on September 30, 1846, inhaled ether from a handkerchief while shut up in his room and seated in his own operating-chair. He speedily lost consciousness, and in seven or eight minutes awoke in possession of the greatest discovery that had ever been revealed to suffering humanity. We can picture the man gradually awakening in his chair

63

first, to the consciousness of his surroundings and then to the consciousness of his great achievement; sitting with his physical frame excited by the influence of the drug which he had inhaled, and his soul stirred to its deepest depth by the expanding thought of the far-reaching effects of what he had done.

"Twilight came on," he said, in subsequently relating the event. "The hour had long passed when it was usual for patients to call. I had just resolved to inhale the ether again and have a tooth extracted under its influence, when a feeble ring was heard at the door. Making a motion to one of my assistants who started to answer the bell, I hastened myself to the door, where I found a man with his face bound up, who seemed to be suffering extremely. 'Doctor,' said he, 'I have a dreadful tooth, but it is so sore I cannot summon courage to have it pulled; can't you mesmerise me?' I need not say that my heart bounded at this question, and that I found it difficult to control my feelings, but putting a great constraint upon myself I expressed my sympathy, and invited him to walk into the office. I examined the tooth, and in the most encouraging manner told the poor sufferer that I had something better than mesmerism, by means of which I could take out his tooth, without giving him pain. He gladly consented, and saturating my handkerchief with ether I gave it to him to inhale. He became unconscious almost immediately. It was dark. Dr. Haydon held the lamp. My assistants were trembling with excitement, apprehending the usual prolonged scream from the patient, while I extracted the firmly-rooted bicuspid tooth. I was so much agitated that I came near throwing the instrument out of the window. But now came a terrible reaction. The wrenching of the tooth had failed to rouse him in the slightest degree; he remained still and motionless as if already in the embrace of death. The terrible thought flashed through my mind that he might be dead—that in my zeal to test my new theory, I might have gone too far, and sacrificed a human life. I trembled under the sense of my responsibility to my Maker, and to my fellowmen. I seized a glass of water and dashed it in the man's face. The result proved most happy. He recovered in a minute, and knew nothing of what had occurred. Seeing us all stand around he appeared bewildered. I instantly, in as calm a tone as I could command, asked, 'Are you ready to have your tooth extracted?' 'Yes,' he answered, in a hesitating voice. 'It is all over,' I said, pointing to a decayed tooth on the floor. 'No,' he shouted, leaping from his chair. The name of the man who thus for the first time underwent an operation under anæsthesia induced by ether was Eben Frost."

The nature of the agent used by Morton was kept secret only a short period; the steps he took to bring his discovery before the medical profession would have rendered it difficult if not impossible, even if ether had not a penetrating tell-tale odour. Morton laid his method before one of the surgical staff of the Massachusetts General Hospital, Boston, the same institution where Wells's ill-managed demonstration had taken place two years before; he requested, with complete confidence, to be allowed to exhibit the powers of his agent. The surgeon was sceptical, but wisely consented, after having satisfied himself that there was no risk to life. A patient suffering from a tumour was chosen, and readily consented to act as a subject for demonstration. A large crowd of professional men and students assembled in the surgical theatre on the morning of October 16, 1846, the day chosen for the trial. The senior hospital surgeon, Dr. J. Collins Warren, was to perform the operation. The spectators, many of whom no doubt recollected the failure with laughing-gas, were disposed to deride when the appointed hour passed and Morton did not appear; but the delay was due only to the desire of the dentist to bring a proper inhaler, and although the crowd received him with a chilling reserve, and the occasion was one fit to try the nerve of the strongest, Morton did not lose his presence of mind. He promptly anæsthetised the patient, and as unconcernedly as does the modern administrator, nodded to the surgeon that the patient was ready. From the first moment that the knife touched the patient, until the operation was concluded, no sound, no movement indicated that he was suffering. The men who had scoffed once and had come, even the surgeon himself, prepared to scoff again, realised the success and the wonder of it, and remained to admire. "Gentlemen, this is no humbug," exclaimed Dr. Warren, as he finished his handiwork. When the patient recovered he was questioned again and again, but stoutly maintained that he had felt no pain—absolutely none. "Gilbert Abbott, aged twenty, painter, single," was the description of the man on whom was performed the first surgical operation under the influence of ether.

News of the great success rapidly spread, and the experiment was repeated by Morton and others in America, and similar work was taken up throughout Europe. It cannot be said that Morton derived much benefit from his discovery. Although the greatness of it was recognised in his lifetime, and he received several honours and presents, he entered into prolonged squabbles concerning the discovery which worried him into a state of ill-health, ending in his death in 1868. A monument was erected over his grave by the citizens of Boston, bearing the following concise description of his achievement:—

"WILLIAM T. G. MORTON,

"Inventor and revealer of anæsthetic inhalation,
By whom pain in surgery was averted and annulled;
Before whom in all time surgery was agony,
Since whom Science has control of Pain."

Whilst the discoverer of nitrous-oxide anæsthesia was dying from chagrin and inaction, and the revealer of anæsthetic inhalation by ether was wasting time in unworthy disputes concerning priority, and fruitless endeavours to gain pecuniary reward, a bolder than either had taken up the work where they had left it, with the high object of pursuing it until he had for ever established the benefit to humanity which he recognised in it. He went straight forwards and onwards, strong in his endeavour; undeterred by the jeers of the ignorant, the opposition of the prejudiced or the attacks of the jealous, with no thought of or wish for reward except that which was to come daily from the depth of sufferers' hearts.

During the Christmas holidays of 1846 Simpson was in London, and discussed the new discovery with Liston, who was one of the first to operate under ether in Great Britain at University College Hospital. The great surgeon thought that the chief application of the process would be in the practice of rapidly operating surgeons; it was at first generally believed that the inhalation could be borne for only a brief period. Simpson speedily showed that no evil resulted if the patient remained under the influence of the vapour for hours. In the month of January, 1847, he gained for the Edinburgh Medical School the proud honour of being the scene of the first use of anæsthetics in obstetric practice. In March of the same year he published a record of cases of parturition in which he had used ether with success; and had a large number of copies of his paper printed and distributed far and wide at home and abroad, so eager was he to popularise amongst the members of his profession the revolutionary practice which he introduced. From the day on which he first used ether in midwifery until the end of his career he constantly used anæsthetics in his practice. He quickly perceived, however, the short-comings of ether, and having satisfied himself that they were unavoidable, he set about his next great step, namely, to discover some substance possessing the advantages without the disadvantages of ether. In the midst of his now immense daily work he gave all his spare time, often only the midnight hours, to testing upon himself the effect of numerous drugs. With the same courage that had filled Morton he sat down alone, or with Dr. George Keith and Dr. Matthews Duncan, his assistants, to inhale substance after substance, often to the real alarm of the household at 52, Queen Street. Appeal was made to scientific chemists to provide drugs hitherto known only as curiosities of the laboratory, and for others that their special knowledge might be able to suggest. The experiments usually took place in the dining-room in the quiet of the evening or the dead of night. The enthusiasts sat at the table and inhaled the particular substance under trial from tumblers or saucers; but the summer of 1847 passed away, and the autumn was commenced before he succeeded in finding any substance which at all fulfilled his requirements. All this time he was battling for anæsthesia, which, particularly in its application to midwifery, was meeting with what appears now as an astonishing amount of opposition, on varying grounds from all sorts and conditions of persons; but the vigour and power of his advocacy and defence of the practice in the days when laughing-gas and ether were the only known agents, were as nothing to that which he exerted after his own discovery at the end of 1847.

The suggestion to try chloroform first came from a Mr. Waldie, a native of Linlithgowshire, settled in Liverpool as a chemist. It was a "curious liquid," discovered and described in 1831 by two chemists, Soubeiran and Liebig, simultaneously but independently. In 1835 its chemical composition was first accurately ascertained by Dumas, the famous French chemist. Simpson was apparently not aware that early in 1847 another French chemist, Flourens, had drawn attention to the effect of chloroform upon animals, or he would probably have hastened to use it upon himself experimentally, instead of putting away the first specimen obtained as unlikely; it was heavy and not volatile looking, and less attractive to him than other substances. How it finally came to be tried is best described in the words of Simpson's colleague and neighbour, Professor Miller, who used to look in every morning at nine o'clock to see how the enthusiasts had fared in the experiments of the previous evening.

"Late one evening, it was the 4th of November, 1847, on returning home after a weary day's labour, Dr. Simpson with his two friends and assistants, Drs. Keith and Duncan, sat down to their somewhat hazardous work in Dr. Simpson's dining-room. Having inhaled several substances, but without much effect, it occurred to Dr. Simpson to try a ponderous material which he had formerly set aside on a lumber-table, and which on account of its great weight he had hitherto regarded as of no likelihood whatever; that happened to be a small bottle of chloroform. It was searched for and recovered from beneath a heap of waste paper. And with each tumbler newly charged, the inhalers resumed their vocation. Immediately an unwonted hilarity seized the party—they became brighteyed, very happy, and very loquacious—expatiating on the delicious aroma of the new fluid. The conversation was of unusual intelligence, and quite charmed the listeners—some ladies of the family and a naval officer, brother-in-law of Dr. Simpson. But suddenly there was a talk of sounds being heard like those of a cotton mill louder and louder; a moment more and then all was quiet—and then crash! On awakening Dr. Simpson's first perception was mental—'This is far stronger and better than ether,' said he to himself. His second was to note that he was prostrate on the floor, and that among the friends about him there was both confusion and alarm. Hearing a noise he turned round and saw Dr. Duncan beneath a chair—his jaw dropped, his eyes staring, his head bent half under him; quite unconscious, and snoring in a most determined and alarming manner. More noise still and much motion. And then his eyes overtook Dr. Keith's feet and legs making valorous attempts to overturn the supper table, or more probably to annihilate everything that was on it. By and by Dr. Simpson having regained his seat, Dr. Duncan having finished his uncomfortable and unrefreshing slumber, and Dr. Keith having come to an arrangement with the table and its contents, the *sederunt* was resumed. Each expressed himself delighted with this new agent, and its inhalation was repeated many times that night—one of the ladies gallantly taking her place and turn at the table—until the supply of chloroform was fairly exhausted."

The lady was Miss Petrie, a niece of Mrs. Simpson's; she folded her arms across her breast as she inhaled the vapour, and fell asleep crying, "I'm an angel! Oh, I'm an angel"! The party sat discussing their sensations, and the merits of the substance long after it was finished; they were unanimous in considering that at last something had been found to surpass ether.

The following morning a manufacturing chemist was pressed into service, and had to burn the midnight oil to meet Simpson's demand for the new substance. So great was Simpson's midwifery practice that he was able to make immediate trial of chloroform, and on November 10th he read a paper to the Medico-Chirurgical Society, describing the nature of his agent, and narrating cases in which he had already successfully used it. "I have never had the pleasure," he said, "of watching over a series of better and more rapid recoveries; nor once witnessed any disagreeable results follow to either mother or child; whilst I have now seen an immense amount of maternal pain and agony saved by its employment. And I most conscientiously believe that the proud mission of the physician is distinctly twofold—namely to alleviate human suffering as well as preserve human life." In a postscript to the same paper he states on November 15th that he had already administered chloroform to about fifty individuals without the slightest bad result, and gives an account of the first surgical cases in which he gave the agent to patients of his friends, Professor Miller and Dr. Duncan, in the Edinburgh Royal Infirmary. "A great collection," he says, "of professional gentlemen and students witnessed the results, and amongst them Professor Dumas, of Paris, the chemist who first ascertained and established the chemical composition of chloroform. He happened to be passing through Edinburgh, and was in no small degree rejoiced to witness the wonderful physiological effects of a substance with whose chemical history his own name was so intimately connected." Four thousand copies of this paper were sold in a few days, and many thousands afterwards.

It is worthy of mention that, according to a promise, Professor Miller had sent for Simpson a few days after the discovery to give chloroform to a patient on whom he was about to perform a major operation; Simpson, however, was unavoidably prevented from attending, and Miller began the operation without him—at the first cut of the knife the patient fainted and died. It is easy to imagine what a blow to Simpson, and to the cause of anæsthesia this would have been had it happened while the patient was under chloroform.

Thus in little more than a year from the date of Morton's discovery of the powers of ether, Simpson had crowned the achievement by the discovery of the equally wonderful and beneficial powers of chloroform. Already he had made two satisfactory answers to the question he had early set himself—first, the application of anæsthesia to midwifery practice; and, second, the discovery of the properties of the more portable and manageable chloroform; the third, and perhaps the greatest, the defence of the practice, and the beating down of the powerful opposition to anæsthesia was yet required to render his reply complete.

CHAPTER VII

The Fight for Anæsthesia. 1847 onwards

His faith in chloroform—Confused public opinion on the subject—Personal attacks—Opposition on professional grounds—His reply—Opposition on moral grounds—His reply—Opposition on religious grounds—His reply—Her Majesty the Queen anæsthetised—Indiscrete supporters—The Edinburgh teaching of anæsthesia administration—The far-reaching effects of the successful introduction of anæsthesia.

Professor Simpson firmly believed that he possessed now in chloroform an anæsthetic agent "more portable, more manageable and powerful, more agreeable to inhale, and less exciting" than ether, and one giving him "greater control and command over the superinduction of the anæsthetic state." Fortified by this belief, full of facts relating to the subject, and fired with zeal and enthusiasm, he was prepared to meet the opposition which from his knowledge of human nature he must have anticipated. So bravely and so emphatically did he champion the cause that he became identified with it in the public mind. The revelation of anæsthesia, the discovery of chloroform, and the application of anæsthetics to surgery as well as to midwifery were attributed to him by all classes of the community, not even excepting many of his own profession. Chloroform was spoken of as if ether had never existed; and chloroform and chloroforming displaced the terms anæsthetic and anæsthetising in ordinary talk—such unwieldy terms were naturally abandoned when there was the excuse that chloroform was universally considered the best substance of its class. Simpson made no attempt as Morton had done to patent his discovery under a fanciful name for his own pecuniary profit; but widely spread abroad every particle of knowledge concerning it that he possessed, so that every practitioner was forthwith enabled to avail himself thereof for the benefit of his patients.

Partly owing to his own enthusiasm and his strong belief in the superiority of chloroform over ether, and partly owing to the confusion prevailing in general circles as to the history of anæsthesia, no small number of attacks were directed against Simpson personally by those who either were jealous of his achievements, or who considered that the part taken by themselves or their friends in the establishment of this new era in medical science had been slighted or overlooked. Simpson took all these as part of the fight into which he had entered. His nature was not sensitive to such personal attacks; he replied to them, cast them off, and went on his way unaffected. He handled some of these opponents somewhat severely when they accused him of encouraging the public belief in him as the discoverer of anæsthesia. It is clear to us to-day after anæsthesia has been on its trial for fifty years that Simpson magnified the superiority of chloroform over ether, and was led by that feeling to look on the history of ether as but a stage in the history of the greater chloroform. He regarded chloroform as the only anæsthetic; his utterances betrayed this feeling, and offence was naturally taken by the introducers and advocates of ether. His opinion of chloroform was shared by the leading European surgeons to such an extent in his day that shortly after his death Professor Gusserow, of Berlin, stated that with a few exceptions almost all over the earth nothing else was used to produce anæsthesia but chloroform.

The real fight for anæsthesia was against those who found in the practice something which ran contrary to their beliefs or principles. There were first those who objected on purely *medical* grounds; secondly, those who took exception to it from a *moral* point of view; and thirdly, those who found their *religious* convictions seriously offended by the new practice.

The *medical* opponents were, perhaps, the most powerful; certainly it was they who had first to be won over, for without the support of the profession the cause was in danger. It was urged first of all that the use of anæsthetics would increase the mortality, then very great, of surgical operations, and those who took their stand upon this ground were men who had at first denied the possibility of making operations painless, and had been driven to abandon that opinion only by a clear demonstration of the fact. To meet this form of opposition he instituted a laborious and extensive statistical investigation in order to compare the results obtained in hospitals where anæsthetics were used with those where the operations were performed on patients in the waking state. He took care that the reports dealt with the same operations under, as nearly as possible, similar conditions in each case. He obtained returns from close upon fifty hospitals in London, Edinburgh, Dublin, and various provincial towns. One of the most fatal operations in those days, and one dreaded by patient and surgeon alike, was amputation of the thigh. In 1845 Professor Syme said that the stern evidence of hospital statistics showed that the average frequency of death after that operation was not less than 60 to 70 per cent., or above one in every two operated upon. Simpson fearlessly collated statistics of this operation amongst the others, and proved that when performed under anæsthetics amputation of the thigh had its mortality reduced to 25 per cent. His figures were as follows:—

Table of the Mortality of Amputations of the Thigh.

	Reporter.	*No. of Cases.*	*No. of Deaths.*	*Percentage of Deaths.*	
Parisian hospitals	Malgaigne	201	126	62 in 100	Not anæsthetised.
Edinburgh hospitals	Peacock	43	21	49 in 100	
General collection	Phillips	987	435	44 in 100	
Glasgow hospitals	Lawrie	127	46	36 in 100	
British hospitals	Simpson	284	107	38 in 100	
Cases on patients in an anæsthetised state		145	37	25 in 100	

He pointed to the above table as a proof that far from increasing the mortality of this operation the introduction of anæsthetics had already led to a saving of from eleven to twenty lives out of every hundred cases. He acknowledged that the number of cases he had collected (145) was somewhat small from a statistical point of view; but he confidently asserted that future figures would show greater triumphs. The tables of other operations showed similar results, and he entered exhaustively into the subject in a paper published in 1848. The paper was entitled, "Does Anæsthesia increase or decrease the mortality attendant upon surgical operations?" According to his wont, he headed it with a quotation from Shakspeare:

"Why doest thou whet thy knife so earnestly?
... Shylock must be merciful.
On what compulsion must I? Tell me that!"

Victorious in this encounter, he turned to those who urged that anæsthetics were responsible for various kinds of ills such as a tendency to hæmorrhage, convulsions, paralysis, pneumonia, and various kinds of inflammatory mischief as well as mental derangement. He combated these contentions until the end of his career; and not only proved that the objections were visionary, but showed that for one of the alleged evils formerly often seen after operations, viz., convulsions, chloroform, far from being a cause, was one of our most powerful remedies.

But the professional opponents of anæsthesia were most emphatic in the denunciation of its use in midwifery. Pain in the process of parturition was, they said, "a desirable, salutary, and conservative manifestation of life-force": neither its violence nor its continuance was productive of injury to the constitution. Strong opposition on these grounds came from the Dublin School, and with characteristic boldness Simpson turned to the statistics of their own lying-in hospital to prove his contention that to abolish parturient pain was to diminish the peril of the process. Again the statistics stood him in good stead; he flourished them triumphantly before his opponents, and proceeded to deal with those who asserted that the use of anæsthetics was accompanied by danger to life. He pointed out that, although unquestionably there were some dangers connected therewith, they were insignificant compared with the dangers in both surgery and midwifery which their use averted. Pain itself was a danger; shock in surgery was responsible for many untimely deaths upon the operating table; by preventing these chloroform saved countless lives. His arguments were characterised by painstaking thoroughness and evidenced wide reading. In addressing Professor Meigs, of Philadelphia, he said:—

"First, I do believe that if improperly and incautiously given, and in some rare idiosyncrasies, ether and chloroform may prove injurious or even fatal—just as opium, calomel, and every other powerful remedy and strong drug will occasionally do. Drinking cold water itself will sometimes produce death. 'It is well known,' says Dr. Taylor, in his excellent work on Medical Jurisprudence, 'that there are *many* cases on record in which cold water, swallowed in large quantity and in an excited state of the system, has led to the destruction of life.' Should we therefore never allay our thirst with cold water? What would the disciples of Father Mathew say to this? But, secondly, you and others have very unnecessary and aggravated fears about the dangers of ether and chloroform, and in the course of experience you will find these fears to be, in a great measure, perfectly ideal and imaginary. But the same fears have, in the first instance, been conjured up against almost all other innovations in medicine and in the common luxuries of life. Cavendish, the secretary to Cardinal Wolsey, tells us in his life of that prelate, that when the cardinal was banished from London to York by his master—that regal Robespierre, Henry the Eighth—*many* of the cardinal's servants refused to go such an enormous journey—'for they were loath to abandon their native country, their parents, wives, and children.' The journey which can *now* be accomplished in six hours was considered then a perfect banishment.... In his Life of Lord Loughborough, John Lord Campbell tells us that when he (the biographer) first travelled from Edinburgh to London in the mail-coach the time had been reduced (from the former twelve or fourteen days) to three nights and two days; 'but,' he adds, 'this new and swift travelling from the Scots to the English capital was wonderful, and I was gravely advised to stop a day at York as several passengers who had gone through without stopping had died of apoplexy from the rapidity of the motion' ('Lives of the Lord Chancellors'). Be assured that many of the cases of apoplexy, &c., &c., alleged to arise from ether and chloroform, have as veritable an etiology as this apoplexy from rapid locomotion, and that a few years hence they will stand in the same light in which we now look back upon the apoplexy from travelling ten miles an hour. And as to the supposed great moral and physical evils and injuries arising from the use of ether and chloroform, they will by and by, I believe, sound much in the same way as the supposed great moral and physical evils and injuries arising from using hackney coaches, which were seriously described by Taylor, the water-poet, two or three centuries ago when these coaches were introduced. Taylor warned his fellow-creatures to avoid them, otherwise 'they would find their bodies tossed, tumbled, rumbled, and jumbled' without mercy. 'The coach,' says he, 'is a close hypocrite, for it hath a cover for knavery; they (the passengers) are carried back to back in it like people surprised by pirates, and moreover it maketh men imitate sea-crabs in being drawn sideways, and altogether it is a dangerous carriage for the commonwealth.' Then he proceeds to call them 'hell-carts,' &c., and vents upon them a great deal of other abuse very much of the same kind and character as that lavished against anæsthetics in our own day."

Following out the same line of reasoning he brought to the minds of medical opponents how the introducers of such useful drugs as mercury, antimony, and cinchona bark had met with now long-forgotten but stubborn opposition; and he reminded surgeons of the stern obstinacy with which the introduction of the ligature of arteries had been long objected to and the barbarous method of arresting bleeding with red-hot irons had been preferred. But in the history of the discovery and introduction of vaccination by Jenner he found a strong parallel; and he wrote a pregnant article to prove that mere opinion and prejudgments were not sufficient to settle the question of the propriety or impropriety of anæsthetic agents, illustrating it from the story of vaccination. The result of vaccination had been to save during the half century since its introduction a number of lives in England alone equal to the whole existing population of Wales; and in Europe during the same period it had preserved a number of lives greater than the whole existing population of Great Britain. And yet Jenner, when he first announced his discovery, had encountered the most determined opposition on the part of many of his professional brethren, who ridiculed and bitterly denounced both him and his discovery; whilst ignorant laymen announced that smallpox was ordained by heaven and vaccination was a daring and profane violation of holy religion. He pointed out that these objections had been slowly and surely crushed out of existence by accumulated facts, and predicted that the ultimate decision concerning anæsthesia would come to be based, not upon impressions, opinions, and prejudices, but upon the evidence of "a sufficient body of accurate and well-ascertained facts." To these facts, as has been indicated, he subsequently successfully appealed.

Those who objected to anæsthesia on *moral* grounds directed their attacks chiefly against its use in midwifery. They not only condemned that application as iniquitous, but went the length of asserting that the birth of past myriads without it proved how unnecessary it was, and that Nature conducted the whole process of birth unaided in a greatly superior manner. The pains associated with parturition were actually beneficial, they said. Simpson answered this by showing that the proper use of anæsthetics shortened parturition, and by diminishing the amount of pain led to more rapid and more perfect recoveries. The leading exponent of the Dublin School of Midwifery at that time foolishly wrote that he did not think any one in Dublin had as yet used anæsthetics in midwifery; that the feeling was very strong against its use in ordinary cases, merely to avert the ordinary amount of pain, which the Almighty had seen fit—and most wisely, no doubt—to allot to natural labour; and in this feeling he (the writer) most heartily concurred. Simpson's private comment on this remarkable epistle at once showed his opinion of it, and ridiculed the objection out of existence. He skilfully parodied the letter thus:—"I do not believe that any one in Dublin has as yet used a carriage in locomotion; the feeling is very strong against its use in ordinary progression, merely to avert the ordinary amount of fatigue which the Almighty has seen fit—and most wisely, no doubt—to allot to natural walking; and in this feeling I heartily and entirely concur."

He twitted the surgeons who opposed him with their sudden discovery, now that anæsthetics were introduced, that there was something really beneficial in the pain and agony caused by their dreaded knife. Such a contention contraverted his cherished principle that the function of the medical man was not only to prolong life, but also to alleviate human sufferings. He quoted authorities of all times to show that pain had been always abhorred by physicians and surgeons, commencing with a reference to Galen's aphorism—"*Dolor dolentibus inutile est*" ("pain is useless to the pained"); citing Ambroise Paré, who said that pain ought to be assuaged because nothing so much dejected the powers of the patient; and, finally, reproducing the words of modern authors, who asserted that, far from being conducive to well-being, pain exhausted the principle of life, and in itself was frequently both dangerous and destructive. He brought forward a collection of cases where in former days patients had died on the operating-table, even before the surgeon had begun his work, so great was the influence of the mere fear of pain; and reminded those who attributed occasional deaths on the operating-table to the influence of the anæsthetic of the numerous cases in bygone days where death occurred whilst the surgeon was at work. He recalled also how the great surgeon of St. Thomas's Hospital, Cheselden, had abhorred the pain which he caused in the process of his work, and longed for

78

some means for its prevention. "No one," said Cheselden, "ever endured more anxiety and sickness before an operation" than himself.

Simpson did not forget to look at the subject from the patient's point of view, and reproduced the letter from an old patient, which has been already quoted (Chapter VI.).

The soldier and sailor, brave unto heroism in facing the enemy, never fearing the death which stared them in the face in its most horrible form whilst answering the call of duty, would quail like children at the mere thought of submitting to the deliberate knife of the surgeon. Were quibbles about the efficacy of pain to stand in the way of the merciful prevention of such suffering by the process of anæsthetisation?

Those who opposed him with this curious idea, that pain after all was beneficial, were some of them men of no mean standing in the profession. Gull, Bransby Cooper, and Nunn were amongst those whom he had to silence. After replying to their arguments *seriatim* with all his polemic power, he referred them once more to the evidence of facts and of facts alone as set forth by his statistics. Had he lived but a twelvemonth longer than he did he would have been able to conjure up a picture of the incalculable amount of suffering prevented by the eighteen hundred pounds of chloroform which were forwarded to the rival armies from one firm of chemists alone during the Franco-Prussian war; happily for the wounded within and around Paris, there was then no longer any doubt as to the propriety of employing anæsthetics.

The *religious* objections to the use of anæsthetics could scarcely be met with statistics. Foolish as they now appear to us after the lapse of time, and with the practice they attempted to repel universally adopted, they were nevertheless urged in good faith by clergy and laity of various denominations. The same kind of bigotry had met the introduction of vaccination, and Simpson himself remembered how many people had opposed the emancipation of the negroes on the ground that they were the lineal descendants of Ham, of whom it was said "a servant of servants shall he be unto his brethren." Sir Walter Scott reminds us, in "Old Mortality," of the spirit which met the introduction of fanners to separate the chaff from the corn, which displaced the ancient method of tossing the corn in the air upon broad shovels. Headrigg reproved Lady Bellenden for allowing the new process to be used on her farm, "thus impiously thwarting the will of Divine Providence by raising a wind for your leddyship's ain particular use by human art, instead of soliciting it by prayer or waiting patiently for whatever dispensation of wind Providence was pleased to send upon the sheeling hill."

To-day in South Africa the same spirit is seen. Honest countryfolk of European descent are earnestly counselled by their spiritual advisers to submit patiently to the plague of locusts on the ground that it comes as a punishment from Providence. These worthy men stolidly witness their cornfields and their grass lands being eaten bare before their eyes in a few hours, whilst their more enlightened neighbours, brought up in another faith, resort with success to all sorts of artifices to ward off the destructive little invaders.

It is pleasant to be able to record that Dr. Chalmers, one of the heroes of Scots religious history, not only countenanced chloroform by witnessing operations performed under it in the Royal Infirmary, but when requested to deal in a magazine article with the theological aspect of anæsthesia refused on the ground that the question had no theological aspect, and advised Simpson and his friends to take no heed of the "small theologians" who advocated such views. This was futile advice to give to one of Professor Simpson's controversial propensities; he entered with keen enjoyment into the fray with these "religious" opponents. His famous pamphlet, entitled, "Answer to the Religious Objections advanced against the employment of Anæsthetic Agents in Midwifery and Surgery," fought his enemies with their own weapons by appealing with consummate skill to Scripture for authority for the practice. The paper was headed with two scriptural verses:—"For every creature of God is good, and nothing to be refused if it be received with thanksgiving" (1 Timothy iv. 4). "Therefore to him that knoweth to do good and doeth it not to him it is sin" (James iv. 17).

The principal standpoint of the religious opponents was the primeval curse upon womanhood to be found in Genesis. Simpson swept the ground from under his opponents' feet by reference to and study of the original Hebrew text. The word translated—"sorrow" ("I will greatly multiply thy sorrow ... in sorrow shalt thou bring forth")—was the same as that rendered as "sorrow" in the curse applied to man ("in sorrow shalt thou eat of it all the days of thy life"). Not only did the Hebrew word thus translated sorrow really mean labour, toil, or physical exertion; but in other parts of the Bible an entirely different Hebrew word was used to express the actual pain incident to parturition. The contention, then, that sorrow in the curse meant pain was valueless. Chloroform relieved the real pain not referred to in the curse, whereas it had no effect upon the sorrow or physical exertion.

If, however, the curse was to be taken literally in its application to woman as these persons averred, and granting for the moment that sorrow did mean pain, their position was entirely illogical. If one part of the curse was to be interpreted literally, so must be the other parts, and this would have a serious effect of a revolutionary nature upon man and the human race all over the face of the earth. Literally speaking, the curse condemned the farmer who pulled up his thorns and thistles, as well as the man who used horses or oxen, water-power, or steam-traction to perform the work by which he earned his bread; for was he not thereby saving the sweat of his face?

Pushed further, the same argument rendered these contentions more absurd and untenable. Man was condemned to die—"dust thou art and unto dust thou shalt return." What right had the physician or surgeon to use his skill to prolong life, at the same time that he conscientiously abstained from the use of anæsthetics on the ground that they obviated pain sent by the Deity? Nay, more; sin itself was the result of the Fall; was not the Church herself erroneously labouring to turn mankind from sin?

In a truer and more serious religious spirit he reminded his foolish opponents of the Christian dispensation, and pointed out how the employment of anæsthesia was in strict consonance with the glorious spirit thereof.

Some persons broadly stated that the new process was unnatural; even these he condescended to answer. "How unnatural," exclaimed an Irish lady, "for you doctors in Edinburgh to take away the pains of your patients." "How unnatural," said he, "it is for you to have swam over from Ireland to Scotland against wind and tide in a steam-boat."

A son of De Quincey in his graduation thesis humorously supported Professor Simpson. He argued that the unmarried woman who opposed

81

anæsthetics on the ground that her sex was condemned by the curse to suffer pains, broke the command herself "in four several ways, according to the following tabular statement":—

"1. She has no conception.

2. She brings forth no children.

3. Her desire is not to her husband.

4. The husband does not rule over her."

De Quincey himself supported his son in a letter appended to the thesis thus:—"If pain when carried to the stage which we call agony or intense struggle amongst vital functions brings with it some danger to life, then it will follow that knowingly to reject a means of mitigating or wholly cancelling the danger now that such means has been discovered and tested, travels on the road towards suicide. It is even worse than an ordinary movement in that direction, because it makes God an accomplice, through the Scriptures, in this suicidal movement, nay, the primal instigator to it, by means of a supposed curse interdicting the use of any means whatever (though revealed by Himself) for annulling that curse."

But the Bible furnished Simpson with the most powerful argument of all in Genesis ii. 21, where it is written: "And the Lord God caused a deep sleep to fall upon Adam; and he slept; and He took one of his ribs and closed up the flesh instead thereof." He strengthened his position by explaining that the word rendered "deep sleep" might more correctly be translated "coma" or "lethargy." He had taken the full measure of his opponents when he answered them with this quotation; it was a reply characteristic of the man, and completely defeated these self-constituted theologians with their own weapons. They had attacked him as a man of science, and found that his knowledge of the Scriptures excelled their own. He did not fail to read these people a lesson, and point out the harm done to true religion by such conduct and arguments as theirs, reminding them that if God had willed pain to be irremovable no possible device of man could ever have removed it.

Such was the great fight—the fight for anæsthesia—which Simpson fought and won. He was the one man who by his own individual effort established the practice of anæsthesia, while Morton has the honour of being the one man without whom anæsthesia might have remained unknown. Such was the opposition encountered, and such was the timidity of his professional brethren, that but for Simpson's courageous efforts it would have been the work of years to bring about what it was granted to him to accomplish in a brief period; if fear, ridicule, contempt, and bigotry had not perhaps sunk the new practice into oblivion. Of the hundreds who are daily mercifully brought under the influence of chloroform and ether, few are aware what they owe to Simpson, even if they know how great is the suffering which they are spared.

Simpson felt that the victory was indeed complete when in April, 1853, he received a letter from Sir James Clark, physician in ordinary to Her Majesty, informing him that the Queen had been brought under the influence of chloroform, and had expressed herself as greatly pleased with the result. It was at the birth of the late Prince Leopold that Her Majesty set her subjects this judicious example.

Much trouble to the cause was occasioned by enthusiasts who administered chloroform with more zeal than discretion, and without any study of the principles laid down by Simpson. As a result of imperfect trials, some persons went the length of saying that there were people whom it was impossible to anæsthetise at all, and others who could be only partially anæsthetised. Wrong methods of administration were used. Simpson patiently corrected these, and carefully instructed his students, so that the young graduates of Edinburgh University carried his teaching and practice into all parts of the world. Syme also took up the cause, and valuable work was done in London by Snow, and later by Clover. The teaching of Simpson and Syme led to such successful results that their methods are followed by the Edinburgh School to this day practically unaltered. So satisfactory an agent is chloroform in Edinburgh hands, that other anæsthetics are in that city but rarely called into requisition. All the world over it is the anæsthetic in which the general practitioner places his trust.

Having seen what Simpson did for anæsthesia, we may briefly review what anæsthesia has done for humanity. That it has entirely abolished the pain attendant upon surgery is easily recognised by the profession and patients alike. The patient never begs for mercy nowadays; he dreads the anæsthetic more than the knife; he has no anxiety as to whether he will feel pain or not, but rather as to whether he will come round when the operation

83

is over; happily after one experience he realises that his fears were unfounded, and, if need be, will submit cheerfully to a second administration.

The horrors of the operating-room referred to in the preceding chapter were vanquished with the pain; the surgeon has no longer to steel himself for the task as formerly, to wear a stern aspect and adopt a harsh manner. The patient has no longer to be held down by assistants; instead of having to be dragged unwillingly to the operating-table—a daily occurrence sickening to the hearts of fellow-patients and students, while it served only to harden the surgeon and the experienced old nurse of those days—he will walk quietly to the room, or submit patiently to be carried there, and at a word from the surgeon prepare

"... to storm

The thick, sweet mystery of chloroform,
The drunken dark, the little death-in-life."

The operation is no longer a race against time; order, method, cleanliness, and silence prevail, where there was formerly disorder, bustle, confusion, dirt, and long-drawn shrieks. Nothing illustrates better the progress of surgery than a picture of the operating-room in the first decade placed beside that of an operating theatre in one of our leading hospitals in this the last decade of the nineteenth century. In the quiet of the patient, in the painlessness of the operation, in the calm deliberation of the operator, and the methodical order of all around him, in the respectful silence that prevails in the room so soon as the patient is laid on the table, we see the direct results of the introduction of anæsthetics. But there are other great, if less direct, results, each making its presence known to the professional spectator. By anæsthesia successful operations previously unheard of and unthought of were made possible after the principle of antiseptic surgery had been established; by anæsthesia experimental research, which has led to numerous beneficent results in practical surgery and medicine, was made possible. Its introduction is an achievement of which the Anglo-Saxon race may well be proud. Wells, Morton, and Simpson are its heroes. The United States has by far the greater share of the honour of its discovery; but to

Scotland is due the glory which comes from the victorious fight. No event in surgery up to 1847 had had such far-reaching effects. Simpson himself looked forward to the discovery of some agent, better than both chloroform and ether; and it is still possible that there may be an even greater future in store for anæsthesia than was ever dreamt of in his philosophy.

CHAPTER VIII

Home Life—Controversies

The foundations of his fame; Comparison with Boerhaave—Family letters—Home amusements—Affection for children—And for animals—Puck—Holidays—Wide area of practice—"The arrows of malignancy"—Squabbles—Homœopathy—Mesmerism—Refuses to leave Edinburgh.

Great as was Simpson's contemporary fame, the chief part of it had its origin in his indescribable personal power over his fellows, and in his inexhaustible energy. When to these was added the reputation won by the discovery of chloroform's anæsthetic properties, he stood not only as the most famous physician of his day, but also as a man marked out for posthumous fame. The personal characteristics of the man were speedily forgotten after his death, save by those who had been brought under their influence; the marked prominence given to Simpson and the "discovery of chloroform" in the numerous recent reviews of Queen Victoria's reign on the occasion of the Diamond Jubilee, indicates that it is by chloroform that Simpson will ever be remembered. His lasting reputation depends on this work, not upon the characteristics which made him famous in the judgment of his contemporaries. The only physician in comparatively modern times, whose reputation approached Simpson's in magnitude was Hermann Boerhaave (1668 to 1738), the Dutch physician, whose fame and influence during his own lifetime were immense. Boerhaave's leading characteristics greatly resembled Simpson's: he had an enormous capacity for acquiring information, and a wonderful facility for imparting instruction to others; his energy and industry were indefatigable, and his memory prodigious. He taught from separate chairs in Leyden the Theory of Medicine, the Practice of Medicine, Botany, Chemistry, and Clinical Medicine, and at the same time carried on his large practice. Patients of both sexes flocked to him from all quarters of the globe, and he is said to have accumulated from his practice a fortune of £200,000 in five and thirty years. Although his treatment and method were, according to our modern knowledge, unscientific, his success in practice was as great as Simpson's; it sprang from the same cause; a wonderful magnetic personal influence, which commanded confidence and faith, so that he succeeded with the same possibly quite simple means which were fruitless in the hands of others. In his day all Europe rang with Boerhaave's name. To-day he is practically unknown. His books are antiquated, and if known, are neglected by modern physicians. He achieved nothing of lasting benefit to humanity. His fate, at least so far as the public is concerned, would undoubtedly have been Simpson's, in spite of his obstetric and gynæcological work, had it not been for the discovery of chloroform.

The increased fame and greatly increased professional income which followed the successful struggle for anæsthesia did not affect Simpson's homely characteristics. He found time in the midst of it all to enjoy the pleasures of home in the society of those he loved best, and of intimate friends. He took a keen delight in quite the smallest enjoyments of the home circle. A characteristic letter was written to his wife in the summer of 1849; she had gone with the children to the Isle of Man; he told her the great and small events of his daily life:—

"Delighted to hear from you that all were so well. Everything goes on nicely here. I have been looking out for a headache (but keep excellently well), for I have been working very busily, and scarcely with enough of sleep. Yesterday *beat* (as Clark writes it) any day I ever yet saw in the house. Did not get out till half-past four, and the drawing-room actually filled beyond the number of chairs and seats! Have had a capital sleep, and got up to look at the ducks; but none laying this morning, so I write instead. To-day I have a fancy to run out to Bathgate, and I think I will.... Yesterday dined with Miller, and Williamson, the Duke of Buccleuch's huntsman, enlightened us about dogs. Miller and I go to Hamilton Palace on Saturday.... My ducks won't lay any more eggs, at which I feel very chagrined.... Two salmon came as presents last week. I gave one to Mrs. Bennet. We are beginning a new batch of examinations at the college. *Such* a sleep as I had yesterday morning! I came home by the last Glasgow train, *very* tired. Tom came to waken me at eight, but I snored so that he didn't. He called me at half-past nine. I don't think I had stirred from the moment I lay down. This morning I have been reading in bed since six. I did not rise till now (half-past seven), because there was no duck laying."

In another letter written on the same occasion he says:—

"... Tell Davie I expect a letter from him. Say to Walter that yesterday Carlo jumped into the carriage after me and saw with me several patients. He usually mounted a chair at the side of each bed and looked in. But Mrs. S. gave him too much encouragement. He leaped into bed altogether and tramped upon a blister! which was very painful."

It was his custom to keep open house at breakfast and luncheon time; but the evening meal was, as a rule, reserved so that he might see and enjoy his own family and intimates. He lived exceedingly plainly himself; he did not smoke; his drink was water: but he delighted in setting a goodly repast before his guests. He loved a romp with his children, and spared an occasional hour from the afternoon for that enjoyment. The same energy entered into his play that was seen in his work. A craze ran through fashionable circles in the fifties for *tableaux vivants*, and was taken up by the Simpson household. He entered with spirit into the new amusement, perhaps more keenly because he saw an opportunity of combining in such representations instruction with amusement. Historical personages and scenes were represented, as well as illustrations of poetry and fiction. With his infective enthusiasm he pressed poets and painters, grave and gay, into service, and there is a record of one highly successful entertainment at 52, Queen Street, in 1854, to which young and old alike were invited. On this occasion most of the scenes represented serious events in Scots history, but Simpson himself seems to have supplied a little comedy. Sandwiched between a scene of "Flora Macdonald watching Prince Charlie" and one of "Rebecca and Eleazar at the Well" came that of "The Babes in the Wood." Simpson and a professional colleague disported themselves as the Babes, and appeared sucking oranges and dressed as children—short dresses, pinafores, frilled drawers, white socks, and children's shoes. They wandered about a while, and then lay weeping down to die to an accompaniment of roars of laughter and to the great delight of the juveniles. It is but a small incident to chronicle, but it shows in his home life the great physician who was beloved by thousands. His deep sympathies made him delight in the society of children. As years increased, and with them work

88

became overwhelming and worries and troubles persistent, he appreciated more and more the refreshment of a frolic with his children. He echoed Longfellow's pure words:—

"Come to me, oh ye children,
For I hear you at your play,
And the questions that perplexed me
Have vanished quite away.

. . . .

For what are all our contrivings,
And the wisdom of our books,
When compared with your caresses
And the gladness of your looks."

His affectionate disposition and kindly manner gained the devotion of his many child patients; and his own family bereavements made him a sympathetic physician and friend to many a sorrowing mother. There was no cant or affectation in his sympathy; it grew out of his large heart.

Animals also he was fond of and gentle to, as we know from the history of the dogs who successively reigned in the household, so charmingly given to us by his daughter. One episode in the life of Puck, a black and tan terrier more intelligent than "breedy," deserves repetition. The dog had accompanied the Professor and some of his children into the country one afternoon on an expedition to dig for antiquarian relics. "After tea Puck, seeing every one carrying something to the station, demanded the honour of relieving his master of a *Lancet*, and went off with his small burden looking very important.... At the station the dog was missing. All got into their places but Puck. 'I will follow in the next train,' said the Professor; 'Puck is too dear a little friend to lose....' All he found of Puck was a muddy *Lancet*, and the last that had been seen of the old dog was that he was pushing his way through a crowd of idle colliers, where it was supposed his energies had been so engrossed in guarding the *Lancet* that he had lost sight of his party.... His master stayed there until next morning, and some remembered afterwards how Puck's loss gave them another evening's talk with one they loved, though he broke in on the reminiscences with 'I wonder where little Puck is,' or 'Is that his bark?' No Puck came to demand entrance, and hope of his return was given up after three days passing without news of him. His master was thinking of the sorrowful letter he would have to write to Puck's companions when late one night, as he paced wearily up and down the room, he thought he heard a faint bark. There had been a great deal of listening of late for the little dog's bark; but it seemed vain to think of Puck's retracing his steps through an unknown country for so many miles. Still the Professor opened the door and called. Up the area steps something did limp into the hall. That it was Puck seemed doubtful at first, for he was quick and bright, and this animal was a lame ball of mud hardly able to crawl. The bright eyes, however, were Puck's; and he confirmed his identity by exerting his remaining energies to give one leap gratefully to kiss the friendly face that bent over him.... His truant play-fellows received a long letter from their father telling them of Puck's adventure and imagining Puck's feelings and trials through his long wanderings.... That letter always recalls Puck and his never-resting master bending over his desk, despite press of business, to send the news to Puck's companions."

Simpson looked no further than his own nursery and circle of close friends for the refreshment and recreation which nature demanded in the course of his busy daily life. But holidays were necessary sometimes. He exhibited all the aversion of an enthusiastically busy man to leaving his work, but would yield sometimes to the solicitations of friends and would more readily leave his patients for a time if a prospect was held out of some interesting archæological research to be indulged in. In 1850 he suffered from an abscess, caused by blood-poisoning contracted during professional work. At the request of his friends Professor Syme was called in, somewhat to the chagrin of Simpson's old friend and colleague, Miller. It is interesting to note that in spite of the recent controversy on anæsthetics, Montgomery of Dublin, who had keenly opposed him, was amongst the first to write a sympathetic note on hearing of his illness; although dissenting from some of Simpson's professional utterances, Montgomery was influenced by the Professor's personality to respect him as a man and a worker.

After this illness Simpson took a rapid run round the Continent, visiting those cities where anything professional was to be picked up. As he expressed it himself he "scampered" round the Universities, Museums, and Hospitals, seeing and hearing all that was to be seen and heard. He stowed away the newly acquired knowledge in the recesses of his mighty brain, and hastened on to the next place of interest before his companions had gained their breath sufficiently to regard with intelligent interest the objects he had already left behind. In Paris, on the occasion of one of his flying visits into a hospital, he was present at an operation, unknown to the surgeon, in which chloroform was used not only as a preventive of pain, but also for its remedial effect; after the operation the surgeon addressed his students upon the subject of chloroform, and Simpson had the pleasure of listening to a hearty eulogy of it. When, at the end, he handed in his card, the operator's delight was genuine and effusive, and the students enthusiastically appreciated the somewhat dramatic scene. On such occasions when he had to submit to the embraces of delighted foreign scientists, the exuberant manner in which they kissed him was not to his liking; even the remote strain of French blood in his own veins did not help him to enjoy the Continental mode of salutation. All over Europe his name was honoured and revered. It is said that when in later years an Edinburgh citizen was presented at the Court of Denmark the King remarked, "You come from Edinburgh? Ah! Sir Simpson was of Edinburgh!"

The last trip to the Continent, indeed his last real holiday, was taken in 1868, when he ran over to Rome. So public was the life he led, such matters of interest to his fellow-countrymen were his comings and goings, that the *Scotsman* newspaper chronicled his doings, relating the sights and places of interest which he visited, and noting that his professional services were taken advantage of by many Roman citizens during the few days that he was there; and that if time had permitted a public reception would have been given to him. In all his foreign trips his object was to learn, not to teach; he followed Sir Isaac Newton's advice to Ashton, and let his discourse be more in queries than in assertions or disputings. He took care neither to seem much wiser nor much more ignorant than his company.

Sometimes feeling the need of rest himself he would take one or perhaps three days for a rapid run to the Lakes, or would spend another in the country unearthing some antiquarian object. It was always a pleasure to him to visit Bathgate, where his uncle and friend Alexander had latterly resigned the baker's business and taken up the *rôle* of banker. One of his favourite resorts was a small house called Viewbank which he had taken, situated on the shores of the Firth of Forth. Here he was close to the fishing village of Newhaven; the fisher folks—the men and the picturesquely attired "fish-wives"—a sturdy and original set of people, were a great interest to him. They knew him well both as an occasional visitor and as the good physician.

One of his letters written in 1856 gives an indication of the wide area over which his services were requisitioned and rendered.

"*Sunday*.

"I write this at Viewbank, which is very pretty this afternoon, but where I have not been for a week or more. This year I have not yet had one single holiday, and scarcely expect one now. I have had many long runs during the past few months. I have been often up in England, professionally, during the summer; once as far as Brighton seeing a consumptive case; once at Scarboro' where my wife went with me; once or twice in London where I saw the Queen; once at Ambleside. I long and weary for a *real* jaunt without a sick patient lying at the end of it. And I had a great fancy to run from Manchester to Douglas and send all the patients far enough; I have been too hard worked to write, but I *must* write one or two papers now. Queen Street has been a little hotel during the summer—always some sick lady or another sleeping in it, sometimes several at night."

Even on these professional journeys he found time to examine objects of interest in the neighbourhood; or if he was unable to leave the immediate proximity of his patient, he brought pen and paper to the bedside and worked while he waited; thus he economised time as he advised his students always to do. It is doubtful if any one less great than Simpson would have ever been allowed to labour thus by a sufferer's bedside; indeed even he was not always permitted to do so. It is recorded that, at least, one lady rose hastily and seized his pen so that he was obliged to desist.

The striking form with which Nature had endowed him, became more remarkable when affected by years, work, and domestic afflictions. Though of medium height his presence, even beside typically large-built and large-boned fellow-countrymen, was never insignificant. His features, overhung by his massive forehead, surrounded by the long and thick hair, spoke his character. Firm, concentrated mouth and piercing eyes, when his mind was fixed on a scientific or practical object. A soft, womanly tenderness about the lips, and a genial, sympathetic emotion in his deep-set eyes when aroused by an object of pity or pleasure. His hand was "broad and powerful, but the fingers were pointed and specially sensitive of touch." To see him was to see one of the sights of the modern Athens. His features are familiar to us to-day as one of the ring of brilliant, intellectual faces forming a frame to the picture of Queen Victoria in this the year of her Diamond Jubilee—a year of triumphant retrospection, unprecedented in the history of nations.

It was impossible that a man holding Simpson's position, engaged in his work, and possessed of distinct fighting characteristics, should not make enemies. He could say, as Jenner said before him, "As for fame, what is it? A gilded butt for ever pierced by the arrows of malignancy. The name of John Hunter stamps this observation with the signature of truth."

The arrows of malignancy did not hurt Simpson. He was very little, if at all, affected by them; but he paid, perhaps, more attention to them than we might have expected him to pay; certainly more than they deserved. His love of the fray led him oftentimes to answer what had better have been left unnoticed, and dragged him into prolonged, sometimes bitter, and, it is to be regretted, often unworthy, controversies. There was so much valuable work to be done, and his efforts were always so fruitful in result that we grudge the time spent in these squabbles; there arises an instinctive feeling that had he devoted the energy wasted in these contests to furthering some single branch of science, he would have made distinct advances therein. There was nothing superficial about his work; whatever the object it was thoroughly entered into; his writings convey to one a sense of the power he had of seeing all round and through a question, and of weighing and judging evidence. There was likewise no scamping in his mode of treating his opponents in these squabbles; he used his weapons fearlessly and administered many a trouncing to weak opponents.

It was a time of upheaval in things medical. The microscope and stethoscope had been introduced into the science and practice of the healing art. Scientific experiment and research were beginning to lay the foundations of rational medicine and surgery. Edinburgh was in the front rank of modern

94

progress, as she has ever been. Men like Simpson, Syme, Miller, Alison, and Christison, were not likely to lag behind. But, unfortunately, it was equally unlikely that such great minds could all think alike in matters concerning the principles of the science and art which they taught and practised. Thus it happened that the Edinburgh School became notorious for its internal quarrels, and in these Simpson was, as a rule, to be found busy.

Quite apart from these professional differences were the disputes arising from attacks made upon Simpson by professional brethren and laymen, who accused him of wrong treatment or neglect of patients. His fame endowed him with almost superhuman powers in the minds of patients and their friends. When all other means had failed Simpson was hastened to as a last but sure resource; bitter the disappointment, bitter was the grief, and also sometimes bitter the things said of him when the anxious friends of a sufferer found that even Simpson's powers of healing were limited. These attacks were some of the "arrows of malignancy," which naturally fell about the over-busy man. He thought it necessary to stop, pick up these arrows, and challenge the assailants; we may regret that he stooped so often to this action, but we feel that it sprang as much from the love of truth and justice as from the dictates of a disposition inclined towards quarrel.

It is impossible to pass over the great controversy which raged in Edinburgh about 1850 on the merits of homœopathy, in which Simpson, of course, took a leading part. About the beginning of the century the practice of medicine by the apothecaries, as the general practitioners were then called, consisted in the most unscientific, nay, haphazard administration of drugs in large quantities and combinations. It was an age of drugging doctors, and the custom had become so thoroughly established that it is doubtful whether any less completely opposite system than that introduced by Hahnemann would have convinced the public that after all so many drugs were not required, nor such large quantities of them. Homœopathic practice was founded on facts improperly interpreted, and laid down for general use a procedure that was applicable in only a limited number of cases. As Dr. Lauder Brunton has recently pointed out, it is in many instances only a method of faith-cure, and as such has its value. The success which its practitioners certainly obtained in many cases where the ordinary wholesale drugging of the day had proved

95

futile, at once made men pause ere allowing their bodies to be made receptacles for the complicated preparations of the physician. In Edinburgh at this time the influence of homœopathy had been felt. Alison, a physician of great renown, was to the end a pronounced polypharmacist, and was said scarcely ever to leave a patient without a new bottle or prescription. Graham, another university professor, was also a thorough-going old school therapeutist. On the other hand, Syme treated all medicine except rhubarb and soda with disdain; and Henderson, the professor of Pathology, and also a practising physician, after professing to consider no medicine of very much value, became a pronounced sceptic, and finally horrified his colleagues by making trials of homœopathy, and gradually becoming enamoured of it until he confessed himself a full follower of Hahnemann's doctrines. Christison was leading the school which urged that the action of medicines should be studied experimentally if their administration was to be founded on scientific grounds. The behaviour of Henderson, who so greatly owed his position as professor to Simpson, stirred the wrath of the latter. He examined and condemned the irrational system of Hahnemann, and threw himself into an attitude of strong opposition. Syme and Christison ably seconded him in strong public action. Henderson was obliged to resign his chair owing to "loss of health." Homœopathy was thoroughly crushed in Edinburgh. The contest between the old system of drugging with large complicated doses of powerful remedies, and the new one of giving on principle infinitesimal doses of the same medicines, served a good purpose. It gave an opportunity for establishing rational therapeutics, a science which is making daily progress, and in the presence of which neither the old system nor homœopathy can stand.

About this same period mesmerism was again coming to the front, this time cloaked as a science termed electro-biology. Simpson acknowledged that there was a great deal in mesmerism demanding scientific investigation; but with his reasoning powers he could not realise the existence of the mystically-termed higher phenomena of animal magnetism, e.g., lucidity, transference of the senses, and, above all, clairvoyance. It happened that a professional mesmerist gave a performance in Edinburgh; learning that the "professor's" daughter was stated to be able to read anything written on paper, or to divine any object enclosed in a sealed box while under her father's mesmeric power, Simpson attended the performance. He took with him a specially-prepared test—a sealed box with certain unknown contents; this he presented at a suitable opportunity. Against their own wishes, but on the insistence of the audience, the performers made an attempt by their methods to detect the nature of the contents of this test-box. They pronounced it to be money; on opening it millet seed was found, and a piece of paper, on which was written, "humbug."

An accusation, couched in bitter terms, that Simpson was really a supporter of mesmerism as it was then known, was published in one of the leading professional journals in London. He indignantly repudiated the suggestion and proposed to settle the matter finally by a simple expedient. He offered to place five sealed boxes each containing a line from Shakspeare written by himself on paper, in the hands of the editor of the journal who had permitted the attack to appear in his columns. To any clairvoyant who read these lines according to the professed method, and to the satisfaction of a committee of eminent medical men, he promised the sum of five hundred pounds. The offer, however, was not accepted.

The brilliant attainments of many of its teachers at this period not only placed the Edinburgh school at the head of the British schools of medicine, but also led to tempting offers being made to individual professors by rival schools anxious to secure their services.

London was a much more lucrative field for practice than the Scots metropolis, and several of the most eminent Edinburgh men had from time to time yielded to the temptation to migrate southwards. Indeed, London as a medical school owes a great deal to the Scotsmen whom she imported. Liston had left for London in 1834, and Syme followed, for a brief period, on Liston's death. In 1848 a strong effort was made to secure Simpson as a lecturer on midwifery at St. Bartholomew's Hospital; without any hesitation he decided to remain in the city where he had fought his way to fame, and where he enjoyed popularity, and a practice sufficiently lucrative to satisfy the most ambitious man. Every patriotic Scot applauded the decision.

During these years of fame and prosperity Simpson concerned himself in schemes for the improvement of the surroundings of the working classes, and helped with speech and purse those who worked among the poor. He strongly supported the establishment of improved dwellings for workpeople and gave much attention to the subject of Cottage Hospitals. He did not neglect the poor amongst whom he had laboured in his early days. He loved old Edinburgh, and the poor inhabitants of it were near his heart. "The Professor" was known in many a "wynd" and "stair," where his services were rendered willingly and without reward.

CHAPTER IX

Archæology—Practice

His versatility—The Lycium of the Muses—The Catstane—Was the Roman Army provided with medical officers?—Weems—His lack of business method—Fees and no fees—Generosity often imposed upon—His unusual method of conducting private practice—The ten-pound note—Simpson and the hotel proprietors.

Professor Simpson's versatility was remarkable. He turned from one subject to another and displayed a mastery over each; it was not merely the knowledge of principles which astonished but the intimate familiarity with details. He was able to discuss almost any subject in literature, science, politics, or theology with its leading exponent on equal terms. He had the power of patient listening as well as the gift of speech; more than that he had the ability to charm speech from others, of making each man reveal his inmost thoughts, betray his most cherished theories, or narrate his most stirring experiences; the most reticent man would not realise until he had left Simpson's presence, that in a brief interview, perhaps the first, he had told his greatest adventures, or laid bare his wildest aspirations before this student of mankind who was summarising his life and character as he spoke. Simpson built up his knowledge not so much from books as by the exercise of his highly developed faculty of observation aided by his memory. He enjoyed the study of his fellowmen and extracted all that was worth knowing from those with whom he came into contact. He never undertook work without a definite object in view, and rarely abandoned his task before that object was accomplished. Quite small researches would lead to considerable and unexpected labour. He preserved his scientific method, his desire to appeal only to the evidence of facts—not to other men's fancies—through his archæological work as well as in more professional lines of study. He laboured long and carefully over such an object as the study of old skulls dug up in antiquarian excursions; setting before himself the object of finding out by the condition and wear of the teeth what kind of food had been consumed by the owners, probably primeval inhabitants of some district. He impressed his methods upon those who worked for him or with him. We find him writing to his nephew, who was about to visit Egypt, telling him when there to gather information as to the suitability of the country for invalids, and directing him how to employ his leisure in furthering this object. He was to study German on the voyage thither, and to take with him as models Clarke's book on Climate and Mitchell's on Algiers, and any French or German books on the subject he might hear of. He would require to collect (1) The average daily temperature; (2) The hygrometric and barometric states daily; (3) The temperature of the Nile; (4) The temperature of any mineral springs; (5) The general character of the geology; (6) The general character of the botany of the country. He asked him to inquire specially as to the effect of the climate on consumption, and pointed out that Pliny described Egypt seventeen centuries ago as the best climate for phthisical patients. For amusement he was to take some good general book on Egypt and Egyptian hieroglyphics. The serious study of a succession of inquirers was to be the young man's holiday amusement!

Simpson's most notable contributions to archæology were made when his time was most occupied professionally. The researches on Leprosy were first enlarged and improved. In 1852, when in the British Museum, his eye was attracted by a small leaden vase bearing a Greek inscription signifying the *Lycium of the Muses*. By a painstaking inquiry he established that this lycium was the *Lykion indikon* of Dioscorides, drug used by ancient Greeks as an application to the eyes in various kinds of ophthalmia. It was obtained from India, and is still used for these purposes in that country. He discovered that there were three other examples of this ancient receptable for the valued eye-medicine in modern museums.

He had correspondents in different parts of Scotland engaged in making researches into antiquities, which he encouraged and directed. Among such were inquiries into the whereabouts of a church said to possess holy earth brought from Rome; and a hunt for ancient cupping-vessels. The work on the Catstane of Kirkliston was elaborate, and a perfect example of his method. Probably this stone, a massive unhewn block of greenstone-trap, had been a familiar object to him in his youth, for it lay alone in a field close

100

to the Linlithgow road. In his monograph he endeavoured to show by close reasoning, with profuse references to forgotten authorities and ancient history, that the stone was the tomb of one Vetta, the grandfather of Hengist and Horsa. His argument ran as follows: The surname Vetta, which figured on the inscription carved upon the stone, was the name of the grandfather of Hengist and Horsa, as given by the oldest genealogists, who described him as the son of Victa. The inscription ran thus: VETTA F(ilius) VICTI. Vetta was an uncommon Saxon name, and no other Vetta, son of Victa, was known in history. Two generations before Hengist and Horsa arrived in England a Saxon host was leagued with the Picts, Scots, and Attacots in fighting a Roman army, and these Saxons were probably commanded by an ancestor of Hengist and Horsa. The battlefield was situated between the two Roman walls, and consequently included the tract where the stone is now placed. The palæographic characters of the inscription indicated that it was carved about the end of the fourth century. Latin (with a very few exceptions in Greek) was the only language known to have been used at that time by Romanised Britons and foreign conquerors for the purpose of inscriptions. The occasional erection of monuments to Saxon leaders is proved by the fact mentioned by Bede that in his time, the eighth century, there stood in Kent a monument commemorating the death of Horsa. In 1659 a writer had described this tomb of Horsa as having been destroyed by "storms and tempests under the conduct of time."

In 1861 Simpson was president of the Society of Antiquaries of Scotland, and delivered an address on the past and present work of archæology which greatly stimulated antiquarian study in his country. Amongst the honours which his antiquarian achievements brought upon him was that of being appointed Professor of Antiquities to the Royal Academy of Scotland; he was also elected a member of the Archæological Societies of Athens, Nassau, and Copenhagen.

He made researches into the subjects of lake dwellings, primeval pottery, and burial urns. One of his most valuable writings was upon the subject, "Was the Roman Army provided with Medical Officers?" He answered the question in the affirmative after a laborious hunt amongst votive and mortuary tablets; no Roman historians had left clear indications of the existence of any army medical department. He found that several tablets were preserved bearing inscriptions referring to army surgeons, which suggested that although they were all known as *medicus* there were degrees of rank amongst them, notably the *medicus legionis* and the *medicus cohortis*. There is a well-preserved tablet in the Newcastle Museum found in that neighbourhood, commemorating a surgeon of the first Tungrian cohort, and one in Dresden, referring to a *medicus duplicatorius*, a term which indicates that the surgeon had been fortunate enough by his attainments to merit, and, we hope, receive double fees for his services.

All his antiquarian study was looked upon by Simpson himself as no more than a relaxation. Fatigued by days and nights of anxious consecutive professional work, he would suddenly dash off for a day into some part of the country where he knew there was a likely "find," leaving patients and students to the care of his assistants. Here he would press into service and infect with his spirit all sorts of local worthies from the squire or laird down to the labourer, who woke up at his stimulation to find that what had been of no concern to them and their fathers before them—perhaps objects of vituperation or superstitious dread—were objects of keen delight and interest, and actually valuable to this astonishing man. Once on a professional visit to Fifeshire he quite casually discovered some remarkable though rough carvings in caves, representing various animals and curious emblems, and he was able to show that they presented features hitherto unnoticed. Fifeshire was famous for its underground dwellings, or, as they are locally called, "weems"—a term which gave origin to the title of the Earldom of Wemyss. After such an excursion he would return to Queen Street full of boyish spirits, eager to narrate his discoveries to interested friends, and refreshed ready to resume the daily round of work. Archæology was his hobby—the hobby on which he rode away for refreshment and relief from the monotony of his life's work; not only did the hobby constantly restore his flagging energies, but as it is given to few men to do, he put new life into his hobby whenever he bestrode it.

In the conduct of his practice he was somewhat negligent. He was one of the old school in these matters; he trusted his head rather than paper, and his head had had such a careful self-imposed training since childhood that it was a good servant. But where the brain has such enormous duties to perform, those which appear to it unimportant must of necessity be comparatively neglected.

Had he been more careful of pounds, shillings, and pence, he would have been more attentive to the details of practice. To Simpson, provided he had sufficient money for all his wants—and his wants were wide, for they included those of many others—pecuniary and business matters were of secondary consideration. In his student days he had lived carefully, accounting, as has been seen, for every trivial expenditure to those to whom he was indebted. But now he was free from the harassing necessity of exercising rigid economy, he cast aside the drudgery of business methods and disdained commercial considerations. He certainly received some very large fees, but the curious mixture of human beings who crowded his waiting-rooms were treated all alike whether they paid princely fees or no fee at all; lots were drawn daily for precedence, and they entered his presence according as they drew. His valet seems to have attained considerable skill in estimating the probable remunerative value of a roomful of waiting patients, and would grumble at night if on emptying the professor's pockets, as was his duty, the result fell short of his calculated anticipations. The man did not approve of the master's habit of giving gratuitous service. There were many who were never asked for a fee, and many others whose proffered guineas were refused. Simpson would not ask for money from those to whom he thought it was a struggle to pay him; the magnitude of his profit-yielding practice rendered this form of charity possible for him; from the really poor he always refused remuneration. His house was filled with all sorts of presents from patients, grateful for benefit conferred, grateful for generosity and consideration. He was also a free giver, and besides supporting orthodox charities made many gifts of goodly sums to persons who appeared to him to be in want, or who succeeded in impressing on him their need for help. He was imposed upon often enough; not seldom by pseudo-scientists full of some great discovery which a little more capital might enable them to complete. Once he corresponded with an enthusiast of this description who confessed that he had been breakfasting on a waistcoat, dining on a shirt, and supping on a pair of tough old leather boots, with the object of finding a

103

solid substance, which combined with lead or tin would form gold—nothing more or less than the time-honoured philosopher's stone! To such a man Simpson gave freely not only once.

To young students entering upon professional life with no other capital than their newly acquired qualifications to practice, he was ever generous. The Scots Universities sent forth many such youths, sturdy and independent, and with feelings that would be easily wounded by any attempt to patronise. But his gentleness, and the sympathy born of his own early experiences and shining in his eyes, made help from him something to be proud of.

It could never be urged against Simpson that he was avaricious. Just as when honours were showered upon him he accepted them with less thought of the personal honour than of the appreciation of his friends and the public, and rejoiced that they were pleased; so he rejoiced in the acquisition of ample means chiefly because of the pleasure he might derive therefrom by helping others.

His method of seeing patients was boldly haphazard; we learn with astonishment that he kept no list of his visits to be made, and started a day's round with only his prodigious memory to guide him as to where he should go. Such a method must have had the result that only cases of interest or urgency were seen. No doubt the able staff of assistants attended to the others, but these comprised not only sufferers from trivial complaints but those afflicted with imaginary ills who had come to see Simpson, not his assistant. Possibly they had already suffered many things of many physicians and were none the better. Such persons blamed Simpson with some reason. In the case of neurotic persons only was his method not reprehensible; continued attendance might have undone the benefit of the one application, if we may so term it, of his strong personality, which sometimes was all that was required, so superstitious was the reverence for his powers. A precise system of registration of engagements and visits ought certainly to have been adopted. We can sympathise with those who felt aggrieved that they could not obtain more attention from the great man, but it must be remembered that by his own method he saw a great number of difficult and dangerous cases, and was able to originate out of his wide and unprecedented experience, modes of treatment which are to-day valued highly and successfully made use of by his professional successors. He never wittingly left a fellow-creature's life in danger, but would hasten at all hours to cases of real urgency.

As is usual where large numbers are striving after the same object some were highly careless in their communications with him. Fees were sent to him with a request for a receipt, but no address was given. Engagements were asked for by persons who neglected to say at what hotel they were staying; and others worried him for letters on quite trivial subjects. On one occasion, it is authentically related, a ten-pound note was forwarded to him by a man who might more reasonably have paid one hundred pounds. The note was somewhat carelessly not acknowledged, and the sender kept writing letters demanding an answer in increasing severity of tone. But he was left to rage in vain. A few nights later Simpson's sleep was disturbed by a rattling window; in the dark he rose and groped for a piece of paper wherewith to stuff the chink and stop the irritating noise. His only comment next morning when his wife, having removed the paper and discovered its nature came to him with it, was, "Oh! it's *that* ten pounds!"

There was a great want of method in all his arrangements, and Dr. Duns confesses to having had considerable difficulty in arranging Simpson's letters and papers, so carelessly were they kept.

The leading hotels in the city benefited by Simpson's reputation. Patients and pilgrims filled their rooms long before tourists began to crowd Scotland as they do to-day. When Simpson was elected to the Chair of Midwifery loud complaints were uttered by the hotel proprietors. His predecessor, Professor Hamilton, had been a man of such wide reputation that they derived much profit from the patients sent in from the surrounding country to be attended by him. How could a young man like Simpson equal this? And yet when he died there was more than one hotel proprietor who could attribute no small measure of his own success to the patients and visitors who crowded not only from the country districts of Scotland but from the most remote parts of the British Empire, as well as from the great cities of Europe and America, to gain help or speech from or perhaps only to see this same Simpson. And his fame had reached the high point it ever after maintained when he was but a young man—before he was forty years of age. It was estimated that no less than eighty thousand pounds per annum was lost to the hotel, lodging, and boarding-house keepers of Edinburgh when he died.

CHAPTER X

PERSONAL—PROFESSORIAL—PROFESSIONAL

His genius—Fertility of resource—Personal influence—Work in obstetrics and gynæcology and surgery—His lecturing and teaching—The healing of wounds—Acupressure—Hospitalism—Proposal to stamp out infectious diseases.

Professor A. R. Simpson has said that his uncle Sir James Simpson's genius showed itself in his power of seeing things, in his power of adapting means to ends, and in his power of making others see what he had seen and do what he had done. We have seen these characteristics displayed in his work upon anæsthesia; it is literally true that he left no stone unturned to gain his end and to make others look upon anæsthesia in the same light as he regarded it. He declared all the while that if he found the opposition to the administration of chloroform in midwifery practice too powerful to conquer alone, he would finally overcome it by bringing about such a state of public opinion on the subject as would compel the profession to adopt his methods.

Whether we regard Simpson as a physician or as a surgeon, as a gynæcologist or as an accoucheur, we find that his success was always due to the same causes. He possessed no secret remedies such as an ignorant and imaginative section of the public often credit to successful medical men. He performed no operations with which other surgeons were not equally familiar and equally capable of performing; indeed he frequently sent his surgical cases to operators in whose hands he considered they would be more skilfully treated than in his. In obstetrics and gynæcology his skill arose not only from his unrivalled experience, but also from his power of rapid diagnosis, and his promptness and boldness in treatment.

His readiness in resource was unfailing. On one occasion, it is related, during an operation the bottle of chloroform was knocked over and its contents were spilled upon the carpet before the surgeon had completed his work; whilst his colleagues were wondering what was to be done or how a further supply of the anæsthetic could be obtained with sufficient speed,

Simpson was on his knees hacking out with his knife the portion of carpet on which the chloroform had just fallen; and by means of this extemporised inhaler the operation proceeded uninterrupted to the end.

He carried his distinguishing energy and thoroughness into every branch of his work; even in extempore speeches made at meetings of professional societies, he placed facts before his listeners in so convincing and lucid a manner out of the extensive variety of his knowledge, and aided by his great memory, that if he did not in reality gain the point he argued in favour of he generally appeared to do so. On such occasions too his imperturbable temper was a valuable weapon.

There is no doubt that the genial professor availed himself fully of the unbounded confidence placed in him by his patients. Those of us who did not know him cannot appreciate what we have already said, that the charm of his personality was one of the greatest factors of his success in practice, and of his social success; there is the risk of the appearance of exaggeration in any description of this personal influence. The sympathy of his heart, a real sympathy, not a thin professional veneer, was made manifest by deed as well as word. It aroused in his patient, quite unconsciously to both, a feeling that this man, above all other men, understood his complaint; that he, the sufferer was the chief, if not the only object of his thought and care. It was said over and over again of him that his words and look did more good than all his physic, so able a wielder was he of that healing power which reaches the body through the mind. Those who knew him not, but falling sick hastened to Edinburgh to be healed by him, were oftentimes cured simply because they felt beforehand that he would cure them. They followed unconsciously the ancient command of the Talmud, where it says, "Honour your physician before you have need of him," and went to him full of respect and fired by faith. Wise men have striven through all ages to take advantage of this influence of the mind over the body, and the necessity of possessing a healthy mind if the body is also to be healthy. A striking proof of the antiquity of the thought has been recently furnished in a fashion that would have delighted Simpson. On a papyrus, dated A.D. 200, brought to light by Egyptian explorers, it is written that Christ said: "A prophet is not acceptable in his own country, neither doth a physician work cures upon them that know him."

The advances which Simpson made in the science and practice of both midwifery and gynæcology were due to the magnitude of his experience and the readiness of his genius to profit by experience. His one thought being the relief of suffering and the prolongation of life, he approached the bedside as a man with less high aspirations would fail to do. He considered only the patient's interest, and gave his genius free play. He took midwifery and gynæcology by storm, and urged them on to great developments; he believed in observing, helping, or imitating nature rather than acting, as his predecessors had done, upon preconceived ideas which oftener than not ran contrary to nature's commands. He avoided meddlesomeness, and stepped in only as the ally of nature. He took numerous hints from bygone practitioners and writers, and developed them. To-day we are profiting by his teaching, and the instruments which he devised or perfected.

To mention all his suggestions and all his contributions to the arts which he specially practised would here be obviously impossible as well as out of place; but to medical readers the mention of one instrument associated with his name, and known as *the sound*, will give a small indication of how much we are in his debt. The principle of this instrument had been known long before he took it in hand, but it was left for him to introduce it into practice, perfect it, and preach its value in diagnosis and treatment. So thorough was his work, so farseeing his science, that our knowledge of its utility has scarcely been added to since he first drew attention to it in 1843.

Towards operative work his attitude was characteristically conscientious. We are told that he habitually put the following question to himself when contemplating a serious operation: "Am I conscientiously entitled to inflict deliberately upon my fellow-creature with my own hands the imminent and immediate chance of death for the problematic and prospective chance of his future improved health and prolonged life?" The fact that he habitually thus questioned himself is an evidence of the state of surgery at that time. Operations were undertaken only as a last resource to save life; the surgeon knew full well that he placed his patient in further peril merely by cutting through the skin, in a manner which has now happily become a thing of the past.

His work was so pre-eminently practical that he never stopped to collect together his experiences into a scientific treatise. Although he revivified midwifery, and was one of the original founders of gynæcology, he left to aftercomers the labour of studying what he had done, and drawing the conclusions on which to strengthen the fabric of the science. His pamphlets, papers, and reports are very numerous. It would be wrong to say that modern thought has approved all that he wrote; but however much time and increased knowledge may have modified his teaching, they have not detracted from the value of his researches, discoveries, and suggestions, or from the stimulating influence of his work upon contemporary practice and thought.

As a lecturer and teacher Simpson succeeded as in the other branches of his work. His brilliant exposition of his subjects and his careful practical manner of teaching his young listeners doubled the fame which had begun with his predecessor, Professor Hamilton, and has ever since belonged to the Edinburgh school of obstetricians. But here again his personal attractiveness and power gained for him the greater part of his success. In the words of the *Lancet*, written when reviewing a posthumous collection of some of his writings, his lectures used to brighten the gloomy days of the Edinburgh winter; in perusing the publication under review, Edinburgh men would "almost think they saw the big head and face of the great obstetrician, as they used to see him beaming with satisfaction or twinkling with genial humour as he told a good story, or related a happy case, illustrative of his own bold and original practice." Both as a lecturer and as a bedside teacher he captured his students by the charm of his diction, the wide range of his knowledge, and as Professor Gusserow has pointed out in his masterly memoir, by his peculiar talent of having his knowledge at his fingers' ends, and that often in very remote details.

Year by year he never failed to obtain the affection of his students; scarcely a man that had been taught by him but would proudly boast that he was his friend as well as his teacher. He treated his large class in a confiding spirit—not as the superior person delivering *ex cathedrâ* utterances, but as the friend rejoicing in his function of admitting those around him into the knowledge in which he seemed to revel. He had a happy method of getting on good terms with his audience before proceeding to the serious business of the lecture. When his health began to fail he was sometimes unwillingly laid aside, and the lectures were delivered by a substitute. On one occasion he re-appeared pale, weak, and lame, after such an enforced holiday, and was greeted enthusiastically by a crowded class. He told them that his servant had said to him that a rumour was abroad that he was in Morningside Asylum. He had asked what answer he had made, and heard that he had replied that so far from being wrong in his mind his master was writing a book in bed. While he did not say that this answer was strictly correct, he was happy to assure them, his pupils, that he was quite right in his mind, although a friend had hinted that morning that he was rather weak in his *understanding*!

Old fellow-students meeting each other in after life as staid practitioners take pleasure in recalling the idiosyncrasies and peculiarities of their teachers; it is probable that no professor has ever been talked over with the appreciation which breathes through the reminiscences of Simpson conjured up by those whom he taught.

Simpson left his mark in other departments besides those of the subject of his professorial chair and of anæsthesia. About ten years after the introduction of chloroform he turned his attention to the process of wound-healing—the repair of necessary wounds inflicted by surgeons in the course of their work—and although he was promptly told to go back to his midwifery, he worked persistently at the subject. In those days the subject was the most burning one in surgery and the methods employed to bring about successful results varied in different schools. The object of all methods was the same, viz., to obtain a healthy, clean, and sightly result after an operation; to leave the part which had been of necessity cut in a condition as nearly as possible approaching that in which it had been found, without the incidence of any of the too frequent grave complications. Surgeons did not recognise at first the power of nature to effect for them what they strove after; they thought to attain their object by compelling the tissues to heal as they desired by complicated applications, and many were the layers of ointments and masses of dressings heaped on wounds for this purpose. For a long time all efforts were directed to the discovery of some specific substance, the application of which would give the necessary impulse towards healing in the desired manner. Before Simpson's day it had been generally

111

recognised that the cause—but its nature was quite undreamt of—of the trouble lay in the air surrounding the wound, and more dressings were piled on to keep out the air. But at the same time bleeding was arrested by tying the cut arteries with ligatures—chiefly silken—and these were left with long ends hanging out of the wound to work their way out by a process of ulceration, or irritation of the tissues until liberty was obtained. This process was practically incompatible with the ideal form of healing, known as healing by *first intention, i.e.*, union without appreciable loss of substance or the formation of *pus* or matter. So-called "surgical fever," secondary hæmorrhage, and blood-poisoning were the frequent fatal results of operation wounds treated in this manner. Simpson and others thought to prevent these alarming diseases by devising other means of closing the arteries; thinking that if some method or material were used, which nature resented less, the wound would more readily close by first intention. In 1858 Simpson stated that he had for some time past been experimenting with substitutes for the ordinary silk and thread ligatures, and in the course of his experiments had made use of iron, silver, and platinum wires. In his usual way he hunted up old authorities, and found a record of both silver and gold threads having been experimentally used by bygone practitioners. He seems to have been pleased with his results, stating that he found the tissues much more tolerant of these metallic ligatures than they were of the ordinary organic ones; that only "adhesive inflammation," not ulcerative suppurative inflammation, was excited. This success, however, was probably due to the superior cleanliness of the metal, but this he did not recognise; had he done so he might have been led to strive after surgical cleanliness, and have partly anticipated the great work done subsequently by others. He went off, however, on a different line, and searched for some readier method of using metallic means of closing the blood vessels, being stimulated by the desire to abolish ligatures altogether. Thus he was led, after ten years' careful research, to the introduction of a method entirely original—that of *Acupressure.* This consisted in the introduction of a fine needle through the tissues across the course of the artery, so that while the needle pressed upon one side of the artery the resisting tissues of the body exerted counter-pressure on the opposite side. He claimed for his method the merits of simplicity, elegance, and cleanliness,

112

and urged that not only did the tissues tolerate the needle as they did not tolerate silk or hemp, but that unlike the ligature the needle could be withdrawn as soon as nature had closed the blood vessel by the process of coagulation of the blood within it set up by the pressure; thus the prolonged irritating presence of a body within the wound which delayed healing until it had ulcerated its way out was rendered unnecessary, and a better and more rapid result was attained. He verified his theoretical considerations by experiments on animals and in one or two operations on the human subject, and in 1859 read a communication on the subject to the Royal Society of Edinburgh.

The paper was written under great pressure of work, indeed he stated that at that time he was hardly ever able to write except when himself "confined"; it was hastily prepared to take the place of that of another Fellow which had failed to be forthcoming a few days before the appointed meeting. It was composed at a country house where he had to sleep for two or three nights watching a case of diphtheria. It was headed as usual by a Shakspearian quotation, this time briefly in Justice Shallow's words, thus:—"Tut, a pin!" On the evening of its delivery an abstract of the paper was forwarded to the leading surgeons in England, Europe, and America, and diverse were the opinions expressed.

In Scotland the new method met with the greatest favour and the strongest opposition at one and the same time. Throughout Europe and America it was everywhere received with applause and support. Excellent results were obtained when the method was properly applied, but technical considerations, particularly the difficulty of using it upon blood vessels far removed from the surface, rendered it unsuitable for universal application.

Professor Syme met the innovation with vehement opposition; possibly he resented this intrusion of the gynæcologist into the regions of general surgery. He took into his class-room one pamphlet on the subject by Simpson, which had especially aroused his wrath; he stormed at the author before his students for "his vulgar insolence," and then, in a dramatic scene, expressed the violence of his contempt by savagely tearing the pamphlet into pieces and casting it away. In a subsequent controversy between these two old opponents, who had been temporarily united by Simpson's conduct in

113

consulting Syme professionally, by their joint action against homœopathy, and by Simpson's defence of Syme when publicly attacked by an English surgeon, the feud was renewed.

Simpson persisted for years in collecting reports of operations in which acupressure was employed, and published them from time to time in the *British Medical Journal* and elsewhere. In 1864 his work on the subject took the form of a volume containing 580 quarto pages. His friends endeavoured to rank acupressure with chloroform as one of the blessings to humanity made manifest by him. He himself recognised that he had failed to gain for acupressure a place in practice such as he had gained for chloroform, but he looked forward to a time, perhaps a quarter of a century distant, when his method would be beginning to be thought about. In this he was mistaken for, on the contrary, acupressure was beginning to be forgotten long before twenty-five years had elapsed. Another worker on more strictly scientific lines had by that time made healing by first intention, without complications, the rule instead of the exception, and conferred a benefit on humanity as great if not greater than that of anæsthesia. In 1867, while Simpson was still alive, Mr. (now Lord) Lister (then a hospital surgeon in Glasgow, and subsequently Syme's successor in Edinburgh) enunciated the new principle of "antiseptic surgery," which recognised the living infective micro-organisms of the air as the cause of the trouble in wounds. He directed that as these invisible organisms (known only by means of the microscope) were present everywhere in the air, found their way into all sorts of wounds, and set up the decomposition which led to disastrous results, they were to be destroyed or excluded from wounds; and he suggested effective means of accomplishing this end. He further abolished the long ligatures which irritated by their presence, and by the organisms they conveyed into the wound when imperfectly cleansed as they usually were; and substituted non-irritating ligatures which nature herself was able to remove by the process of absorption. The recognition of this antiseptic principle effected a much needed revolution in surgery, and in this revolution acupressure was practically annihilated. Simpson did not live long enough to see the complete establishment of the Listerian principle; at first he vigorously opposed what he considered to be an attempt to retain the old-fashioned ligatures in

114

preference to his new acupressure; but with his penetrative eye he must have foreseen that should the new practice prevail and short absorbable ligatures be made possible, acupressure would be completely superseded.

In the estimation of the writer of the obituary notice of Professor Simpson in the *British Medical Journal*, the greatest of all his works was that undertaken in the subject of Hospitalism. As early as 1847 he had been horrified to read in a report of the work done in the Edinburgh Infirmary, that out of eighteen cases of primary amputation performed during a period of four years only two survived. He faced this fact with the courage of the reformer, and sought far and near for other facts to support the theory which he gradually evolved, that this melancholy failure of surgeons to save their patients' lives was due not so much to the operation or the operator as to the environment of the patient. In later years he himself often shrank, on account of unfortunate experiences, from performing capital operations which he had formerly unhesitatingly undertaken. The unhealthiness of hospitals had long been recognised; and was especially observed at times when they were overcrowded, as happened during war time. When the public had thoroughly grasped the utility of anæsthetics, and recognised that operations could be performed painlessly, there were fewer refusals to submit to the knife; there was a rush to the hospitals, and the surgical wards throughout the length and breadth of the land became crowded with men and women actually longing for operation. Amongst these all the dreaded sequelæ of surgical interference, which no power seemed able to check, ravaged with alarming severity.

It is to Simpson's credit that he perceived how the introduction of anæsthesia had taxed the hospitals and bewildered the operators, who sought diligently but unsuccessfully in every direction for some means of reducing hospital mortality. He was one of the first to set to work with method to investigate this question of Hospitalism.

It was towards the end of his career, when the old Edinburgh Infirmary stood condemned, and various proposals for rebuilding it on a new site and improved plan were under discussion, that his voice was most loudly heard. For many years he had thought and taught that the great mortality after operations in hospitals was due to the impure state of the air therein, derived from the congregation of a large number of sick persons under one roof. He picturesquely stated that the man laid on a hospital operating table was exposed to more chances of death than the English soldier was on the field of Waterloo. His original suggestion was that hospitals might be changed from being crowded palaces, with a layer of sick on each floor, into villages or cottages, with one, or at most two, patients in each room; the building to be of iron, so that it could be periodically taken down and reconstructed, and presumably thoroughly renovated. This drastic proposal brings nowadays a smile to the lips, for we see now how he was groping in the dark; but the magnitude of it is but the shadow of the evil it was designed to cure. The change was so great as to be impracticable in the eyes of most men; he, on the other hand, contended that it was to be of incalculable benefit to humanity, and, therefore, no difficulty, however great, should be allowed to stand in the way. He did not understand that the evils arose not from the air itself but from what was in the air, known to us now as the micro-organisms. His remedy was a proposal to run away from the evils without receiving any guarantee that they could not and would not successfully pursue. Had Lister not arisen, Simpson's proposals might have possibly prevailed, for he laboured with all his persistent energy.

The general belief of the profession—but it was no more than a belief—was that operations performed in country practice were not so frightfully fatal as those performed in town hospitals. This was Simpson's opinion, and he determined to test its truth by appeal to facts. He drew up a circular with a schedule for the insertion of results in a statistical form, and sent it far and wide amongst country practitioners. He awaited the result with anxious expectation; the circular asked for a plain statement of facts only, and for all he knew the facts might be against his theory; but they were not. From all over England and Scotland, particularly from mining districts, where severe operations after accidents were common, the filled-up schedules flowed in, to the number of 374. These were collected, carefully classified and summarised. The operations selected were amputations, and the result briefly was this:—

Total number of cases 2,098 } Mortality, 10.8 per cent. Total number of deaths 226   The relative mortality of the different amputations was also shown:—

Cases. Deaths. Mortality.

per cent.   Thigh 669 123 18.3 Leg 618 82 13.2 Arm 433 19 4.3 Forearm 378 2 0.5   The table on the next page compared the results of operations for injury with those performed for disease.

For Injury.

Cases. Deaths. Mortality.

per cent.   **Thigh 313 80 25.5 Leg 409 57 13.4 Arm 344 14 4.0 Forearm 313 2 0.6 For Disease.**

Cases. Deaths. Mortality.

per cent.   Thigh 356 43 12.0 Leg 209 25 12.0 Arm 89 5 5.6 Forearm 60 0 —   These statistics were accompanied by an exhaustive detailed examination and explanation; every possible point of attack was considered and protected. "I doubt not," he said, "that the segregation of the sick from the sick—every diseased man being a focus of more or less danger to the diseased around him—is a principle of no small moment and value." He attributed the comparative brilliancy of these statistical results to the *isolation* of the patients only; he endeavoured to show that the operations were often performed amidst dirty and squalid surroundings, on dirty and squalid persons. He did not attribute sufficient importance to the fact urged by many of his correspondents, who supported his general contentions almost to a man out of their own experience, that where fresh air, ventilation, and cleanliness prevailed, the results were always the most satisfactory.

The next step was to take hospital statistics of similar operations, and the general result appears in the table on page 183.

This testimony to the truth of Simpson's opinion was more pronounced than even he himself had anticipated. "Shall this pitiless and deliberate sacrifice of human life to conditions which are more or less preventable be continued, or arrested? Do not these terrible figures plead eloquently and clamantly for a revision and reform of our existing hospital system?" This was his cry until at length breath failed him. The opposition was not strong, but the support was weak. Although there was much criticism, his conclusions were scarcely called in question at all; trifling holes were picked in his statistics, but his contentions were universally acknowledged to be correct; a few reformers only, persuaded as he was of the evils of hospitalism and working at the subject, lent him their advocacy. But he alone stood unperturbed at the extent of the evils and the magnitude of the change which he proposed in order to uproot them; death laid him low as he stood, but not before he had modified his proposals by suggesting that existing hospitals might be reconstructed, and new hospitals built on the now almost universally adopted pavilion system on which the new Edinburgh Royal Infirmary was one of the first to be built.

HOSPITAL.	FOR INJURY.								FOR DISEASE.							
	Thigh		Leg		Arm		Forearm		Thigh		Leg		Arm		Forearm	
	Cases	Deaths	Cases	Deaths	Cases	Deaths	Cases	Deaths	Cases	Deaths	Cases	Deaths	Cases	Deaths	Cases	Deaths
Edinburgh Infirmary	65	48	58	29	21	12	39	5	134	48	28	9	7	3	19	7
Glasgow Infirmary	100	60	93	50	101	38	66	9	177	68	82	27	23	6	19	1
Nine London Hospitals	139	88	179	102	97	33	64	11	320	123	173	53	48	13	37	7
Total	304	196	330	181	219	88	169	25	631	239	283	89	78	22	75	15
Mortality per cent.																

64.4 54.8 40.1 14.8 37.8 31.4 28.2 2.O   The total number of cases 2,089 } mortality 41 per cent. The total number of deaths 855 Placed side by side the Town (hospital only) and Country (private practice only) figures compared as follows:— *Hospital* 2,089 cases 855 deaths 41 per cent. mortality or 1 in 2.4 *Country* 2,098 cases 226 deaths 10.8 per cent. mortality or 1 in 9.2   The steady advance of aseptic surgery has slowly but surely brought about the results which Simpson strove to attain by a radical measure. The enemy which had baffled surgeons for centuries was revealed by Lister. He sent surgeons smiling into the operating-room practically certain of success instead of dreading the terrible onslaught upon their own handiwork of the formerly unseen and unknown destroyer. The death rate of operations is being daily brought nearer and nearer to vanishing point. In his review of the progress of wound treatment during the Victorian Era published in the Diamond Jubilee number of *The Practitioner*, Mr. Watson Cheyne says the mortality of major operations does not now exceed in hospitals more than three or four per cent., and this is made up practically entirely by cases admitted almost moribund and operated on *in extremis* with faint hope of survival. The field of surgery, too, has been vastly enlarged, and the term "major operation" includes not merely operations of necessity, undertaken through ages past as the only possible means of saving life, but also operations which have become possible only in recent years—some of them performed merely to make the patient "more comfortable," or even only "more beautiful." And this glorious result is due, as Mr. Cheyne truly says, to the immortal genius of Lister.

In 1867 Simpson propounded in the *Medical Times and Gazette* a proposal for stamping out smallpox and other infectious diseases such as scarlet fever and measles. In spite of vaccination, which, however, was imperfectly carried out, smallpox alone carried off five thousand lives annually in Great Britain. A serious outbreak of rinderpest in the British Islands amongst cattle had recently been arrested and exterminated by the slaughter of all affected animals. The disease spread as smallpox did by contagion, and Simpson fell to wondering why smallpox could not also be exterminated. His paper was a noteworthy contribution to the then infant science of Public Health, and his proposal, which was, however, universally regarded as impracticable, sprang from his courageous enthusiasm as did that concerning hospitals. He suggested that the place of the pole-axe in the extermination of rinderpest might in the arrest of smallpox be taken by complete isolation, and he laid down simple but rigid rules for its enforcement. An attempt was made to utilise these a few years after when an epidemic of fatal violence broke out in Edinburgh. He was in no way an anti-vaccinationist, but his isolation measures were too strong for the people in those days. We are not surprised that he boldly proposed this measure, for he related glaring instances of neglect of the simplest precautions. Beggars held up infants with faces encrusted with active smallpox into the very faces of passers-by in the streets of Edinburgh; and on one occasion a woman was found in Glasgow serving out sweetmeats to the children of a school with her hands and face covered by the disease. He cried aloud for legislation to prevent such gross abuses, which he did not hesitate to stigmatise as little short of criminal.

CHAPTER XI

FURTHER REFORMS—HONOURS

Professional and University Reform—Medical women—Honours—The Imperial Academy of Medicine of France—Baronetcy—Domestic bereavement—The University Principalship—Freedom of the City of Edinburgh—Bigelow of Boston—Views on education—Graduation addresses.

Professor Simpson took a warm interest in medical politics, and made himself heard as a member of the Senatus of the University. That body was not renowned for any spirit of harmony prevailing in its midst; it included the medical professors many of whom were in professional opposition to each other and were actuated by conflicting interests. The rivalry prevailing amongst the leaders of the profession in the Scots capital was amusingly shown in one of Sir James's letters, where he related how Professor Miller had just given a capital address to the young graduates and recommended them to marry chiefly because Mr. Syme had advised the reverse two years before. "At least," he said, "so Mr. Syme whispered to me, and so, indeed, did Miller himself state to Dr. Laycock!"

On the principles of Medical Reform and University Reform the professors were, however, practically unanimous, but their interests came into conflict with those of the extra-academical school. The two opposing bodies worked hard to gain their own ends when a Parliamentary Committee was appointed in 1852 to inquire into medical reform. The modern Athens became once more disturbed by wordy warfare. The general ends aimed at by the reformers were the obtaining of a proper standing for qualified practitioners; some satisfactory means of enabling the public to distinguish between regular and irregular, quack, practitioners; and to define the amount of general and professional knowledge necessary for degrees and qualifications. It was also desired to remove the absurd anomaly whereby, although Scots medical education was then ahead of English, Scots graduates had no legal standing in England. The Medical Act which was passed in 1858 carried out many of the best suggestions made before the Committee, and effected desirable improvements both in the status of practitioners and in medical education; but it was inadequate, as time has shown, and the question of reform still burns. Simpson took an active interest in the proceedings before the Committee, and made several dashes up to London to further the projects which he had at heart. The annual meeting of the British Medical Association was held in Edinburgh in July, 1858, at the moment when the fate of the Bill hung in the balance. As the journal of the Association said at the time the fruit of a quarter of a century's growth was plucked in the midst of the rejoicings. Sir Robert Christison publicly stated that owing to Simpson's energetic efforts certain far-reaching and objectionable clauses, which had been allowed to creep into the Bill, were expunged at the last moment. Simpson went up to London by the night train, employed the following day in effecting his purpose, and returned the next night; this was when the journey took nearly twice as many hours as now.

The Universities (Scotland) Act was also passed in 1858; by it the complete control of the University, and with it the patronage of many of the Chairs, was lost to its original founders, the Town Council, who had so carefully and successfully guided it through nearly three centuries. The Council did not part from their charge without a struggle; in urging their cause they proudly pointed to the fact that they had appointed Simpson to the Chair of Midwifery against the opposition of the medical faculty. To have elected him, they thought, under such circumstances displayed their discernment, vindicated their existence, and pleaded for the perpetuation of their elective office.

When the question of the admission of women to the study of medicine came up in Edinburgh and divided the ancient city once more into two hostile camps, Simpson's sympathies appear to have gone with the sex to which he was already a benefactor. He recognised that there was a place, if a small one, within the ranks of the profession for women; and when the question came to the vote he cast his in their favour. The proposal, however, was rejected, and has only quite recently become law in the University.

Numerous honours were heaped upon him during the last five-and-twenty years of his life. In 1847 he filled the office of President of the Edinburgh College of Physicians, and in 1852 held the corresponding post in the Medico-Chirurgical Society. In the following year the Imperial Academy of Medicine of France—a body which lacks an analogue in this country—conferred upon him the title of Foreign Associate. This was a jealously guarded honour awarded only to the most highly distinguished men of the day, and it was conferred upon Simpson in an altogether unprecedented manner which doubled its value. According to custom a commission of members prepared a list of renowned men whom they advised the Academy to elect; in the list no British name appeared although Owen, Faraday, and Bright were entered as "reserves." On the day of election the members accepted all the candidates named in the original list until the last was reached. When the president asked for the vote for this individual a sensational and truly Gallic scene was enacted. Almost to a man the members rose, and loud and long proclaimed Simpson's name. Excited speeches were made, and amidst great enthusiasm he was elected to the one remaining vacancy by an overwhelming majority. It had remained for Simpson to prove, as the President courteously pointed out at the time, that there existed a greater honour than that of being elected by the Academy—viz., that of being chosen in *spite* of the will of the Academy itself.

This was by no means the only honour awarded to him by France. In 1856 the French Academy of Sciences voted him the Monthyon Prize of two thousand francs for "the most important benefits done to humanity." Other foreign societies added their compliments, and he was elected Foreign Associate of the Belgian Royal Academy of Medicine, of the Parisian Surgical and Biological Societies, and of the Medical Societies of Norway, Stockholm, Copenhagen, New York, Massachusetts, Leipsic, and other places.

In 1866 his own country made an acknowledgment of his eminent attainments when the Queen offered him a baronetcy on the advice of Lord John Russell. Twice before he had refused a title, but this time he wrote to his brother that he feared he *must* accept although it appeared so absurd to take a title. This honour was the first of its kind ever conferred upon a doctor, or even upon a professor, in Scotland. It was entirely unsought, and scarcely welcomed by its recipient for its own sake; he regarded it not merely as a personal honour but also as a tardy recognition of the services of the

Edinburgh school in the cause of medicine. He enjoyed the congratulations which showered upon him, and felt glad when the citizens flocked to Queen Street to express their feelings, much to Lady Simpson's delight. The medical papers unanimously approved of the honour, the *Lancet* remarking that apart from his connection with chloroform, Simpson was distinguished as an obstetric practitioner, as a physiologist, as an operator, and as a pathologist of great research and originality.

Domestic bereavement quenched the rejoicings over the baronetcy, and condolences displaced congratulations. He fell ill for a time himself, and in a condition of unusual mental depression spoke of the baronetcy as appearing even more of a bauble in sickness than in health. In less than a fortnight after the offer of the title his eldest son David died after a short illness. He had been educated for the medical profession, and was a youth of considerable promise and of an earnest temperament; his death fell as a severe blow, and Simpson even contemplated abandoning the baronetcy which had not yet been formally conferred. The words of his friends, however, and the thought that his dead son had particularly insisted on its acceptance, persuaded him.

A coat of arms had to be drafted for the new Baronet, and this was a pleasant interest for one of his tastes. The family history was searchingly entered into, and the arms of his father's family were differenced on the most correct lines with those of the Jervays from whom his mother had sprung. In the matter of a crest he was able to be boldly original, and adopted the rod of Æsculapius over the motto *Victo dolore*, and thus handed down to his family the memory of his great victory over pain. In June of the same year, 1866, the University of Oxford conferred upon him one of the few honours which reached him from England in awarding him the honorary degree of Doctor of Civil Law. The University of Dublin made him an honorary Doctor of Medicine, and he was created an honorary Fellow of the King's and Queen's College of Physicians of Ireland.

By the death of the veteran Sir David Brewster, in February, 1868, the office of Principal of Edinburgh University fell vacant. This post is a survival from the earliest days. The College out of which the University grew was established in 1583 by the Town Council under a charter granted by James

VI. Only one regent or tutor was necessary at first to teach the "bairns," as the students were termed in the contract entered into between Rollock, the first regent, and the city fathers. Rollock was promised that as the college increased "in policy and learning" he should be advanced to the highest post created. By his own efforts the number of students increased so greatly that within the first few years several other regents were appointed, and the Council, remembering their promise, dignified him with the title of Principal or First Master in 1586. This office was held during the succeeding two centuries by a series of more or less worthy men, prominent among whom were Leighton, afterwards Archbishop of Glasgow, and William Carstares, better known as a statesman and for his connection with the Rye House Plot in 1684. During Carstares's tenure the tutors were turned into professors, and the college became more strictly speaking a university, although from the first it had assumed without any right by charter the function of degree-granting. Although the utility of the post quite vanished when the college became a university, and the principal had no place in the constitution of a university, nevertheless the principalship was not abolished. The Universities Act of 1858 recognised the office, but only as that of an ornamental head, acting as president of the assembly of professors constituting the Senatus Academicus. The salary is a thousand pounds a year with an official residence, not within the precincts or the University. The former head master of the college, known by and knowing every student, became a sinecurist of whose existence it is no exaggeration to say many of the students are, through no fault of their own, unaware. Brewster had been a distinguished occupant of the post—distinguished not as a principal, for he received the appointment only at the age of seventy-eight, but as a scientist. To the public he was best known as the author of the "Life of Sir Isaac Newton," and as the inventor of the kaleidoscope. It is said that Brewster never spoke as much as five lines at the meetings of the Senatus Academicus without having previously written them down; and it is probable that this lack of spontaneous utterance from the Chairman gave the tone to the assembly. The rival professors doubtless nursed their animosities for some less dignified meeting-place, differing there only on the most correct academic lines.

It is not surprising that Simpson at first refused to be a candidate for

125

the vacant post. He would undoubtedly have made an unrivalled figure-head for his *Alma Mater*; he was the leading figure in Scotland already and "did the hospitalities" of Edinburgh to distinguished visitors of all classes. But he would probably have been obliged to resign his professorship and have thus been cut off from his sphere of greatest usefulness; and although he would have grasped with ease the details of university affairs it is open to question whether he would have suitably filled the post of president over men to many of whom he was in professional opposition. The most that the suggestion that he should be a candidate conveyed was a well-meant compliment, but it would have been a greater compliment on his part if he had really ended his life as the ornamental head of the University he had already done so much to adorn. He would certainly have turned his position to good account, and perhaps might have earned the gratitude of all succeeding students by improving their position in the University and bettering their relationship with their teachers—a much needed reform at that time. But he was a man for more active occupation, and it was more fitting that he should persevere to the end in the work of his life. Simpson expressed his opinion that the most suitable man for the post was the one already named by Brewster and desired by a majority of the Senatus; but that man, Professor Christison, then over seventy years of age, generously said that Sir Alexander Grant, an active candidate, would better fill the post. A strong section of Edinburgh folks persisted in pushing Simpson, and in deference to their wishes he consented to enter the lists. It cannot be said that he displayed any of the eager energy which had marked his candidature for the midwifery chair; but his friends made up for his comparative apathy. They were met by a strong opposition, not instigated by his rivals for the post, but offered by insignificant persons who cherished ill-will against him and spread untrue statements with the object of damaging his character. Greatly owing to the reports spread in this manner he was not elected. Sir Alexander Grant became the new Principal. The fact that he could not gain the post was communicated to him in a letter which reached him one morning before prayers. He conducted the worship as usual after reading the letter, and when the family had afterwards all assembled at the breakfast table he intimated the fact to them and dismissed the subject from his mind with the quiet remark, "I have lost the

Principalship."

An interesting episode pertaining to this period was narrated by the Free Church minister of Newhaven. "The election," he wrote to Dr. Duns, "took place on a Monday, and it was on the Sabbath preceding, between sermons, that one of my people, a fisherman, called on me stating that his wife was apparently dying, but that she and all her friends were longing most intensely for a consultation with Sir James. I did not know well what to do, for I knew that his mind was likely to be very much harassed, and I shrank from adding to his troubles. But in the urgency of the case I wrote him a note simply stating that one of the best women in the town was at the point of death and longed for his help, leaving the matter without another word to himself. The result was that he came down immediately, spent three hours beside his patient, performed, I am told, miracles of skill, and did not leave her till the crisis was over. She would, I am assured, have died that evening, but she was one of the sincerest mourners at his funeral, and she still lives to bless his memory. After all was over he went into a friend's house and threw himself down on a sofa in a state of utter exhaustion. This was the way in which, without hope of fee or reward, and while others were waiting for him able to give him both, Sir James spent the evening preceding the election. Some will say it was no great matter after all. Why, for that part of it, neither was the cup of cold water which the dying Sir Philip Sidney passed from his own lips to those of a wounded soldier in greater agony than himself. But the incident is recalled whenever his name is mentioned as adding to the glory of the knight *sans peur et sans reproche*, and the incident I have mentioned in the Newhaven fisherman's house surely gives to Sir James a place beside him in the glorious order of chivalrous generosity."

Among the last of the honours offered to Simpson was the Freedom of the City of Edinburgh; a fitting tribute from the City in which and for which he had so nobly and untiringly laboured. It was proposed to present him with the burgess-ticket at the same time that it was publicly presented to another hero in a different sphere, Lord Napier of Magdala; but by his own desire the ceremony was postponed so far as he was concerned in order that full honour might be paid to Lord Napier. At the eventual presentation the Lord Provost made a short speech recapitulating the achievements for which they desired to honour him, and referring to his reputation as being great on the banks of the Thames and the Seine, as well as on the shores of the Firth of Forth; he likewise expressed the pride of his fellow-citizens that Sir James had remained amongst them and had not been drawn away like other men of genius before him by the attractions of the greater metropolis of the south. Simpson's reply took the form of an impromptu review of his career from the time he first entered the City as a wonderstruck boy. "I came," he proudly said, "to settle down and fight amongst you a hard and up-hill battle of life for bread and name and fame, and the fact that I stand here before you this day so far testifies that in the arduous struggle I have—won."

The accounts of the speeches delivered on this occasion which reached America raised the indignation of Dr. Bigelow, of Boston. Reference had been made to chloroform in a manner which appeared to slight Morton's work in introducing ether as an anæsthetic before chloroform was heard of. In Bigelow's estimation Simpson posed as a hero at the expense of Morton. Simpson had certainly been far from liberal in his allusions to Morton and others in his article upon Anæsthesia in the *Encyclopædia Britannica*, and had written almost entirely about his own discovery. A controversy was excited, and on his deathbed Simpson wrote a letter to Bigelow to prove that he had duly considered the priority and the value of Morton's and Wells's work. In his concluding sentences he expressed regret at having taken up so much of his own and his correspondent's time in such a petty discussion, but blamed his illness which prevented him from writing with the force and brevity required. "With many of our profession in America," he said, "I have the honour of being personally acquainted, and regard their friendship so very highly that I shall not regret this attempt—my last, perhaps—at professional writing as altogether useless on my part if it tend to fix my name and memory duly in their love and esteem."

The widespread national expression of the sense of loss and of sympathy which reached Edinburgh from the United States after Sir James's death testified to the regard in which he was held from one end to the other of that country. In Boston itself the Gynæcological Society, of which he had been the first honorary member, convened a special memorial meeting, which was solemn and impressive. He had not been mistaken in presuming with his last breath that he held the regard of his American *confrères*.

On the subject of education Simpson held what were considered advanced opinions, but which had already been expressed by Mr. Lowe. A few years before his death he delivered a lecture on Modern and Ancient Languages at Granton, in which he lamented the common neglect of modern languages in the education of the day. He had personally felt the want of a mastery over French and German, both in the course of his studies and during his travels; nor did he feel the want compensated for by his ability to write and talk in Latin. He strongly advocated the paying of more attention to the modern and less to the dead languages, and he urged that natural science should take its place in the ordinary curriculum of the great public schools. These views were used as an argument against his fitness for the post of Principal of the ancient University.

On three separate occasions it fell to Simpson's lot to deliver the annual address to the newly-fledged graduates, which is the duty of the professors of the medical faculty in rotation. This ceremony remains deeply impressed in the memory of Edinburgh men, simple and dull as it undoubtedly is. The homily delivered by the orator of the day contains excellent counsels appropriate to the occasion, but the young man eager to rise and confidently try his wings pays little attention to the words of wisdom; unless it be to feel wonder that just as he is about to leave them, probably for ever, his *Alma Mater* and her priests have discovered an affectionate regard for him and his welfare. A few years later the struggling young practitioner may perhaps turn to the copy of this graduation address, forwarded to him by post with the author's compliments, and find in such an one as Simpson delivered much to strengthen and encourage him. In 1842 and 1855 he delivered addresses from which quotations have already been made; and in the third one, spoken in 1868, he made a forecast of the future of medical science, predicting *inter alia* that by concentration of electric or other lights we should yet be enabled to make many parts of the body sufficiently diaphanous for inspection by the practised eye of the physician. It was his habit to commit such lectures to memory and to deliver them without notes. He was a ready public speaker on any subject in which he was interested; speeches made on the spur of the moment teemed with pleasantly-put facts and apt anecdotes from the vast storehouse of his memory. A speech from Sir James was one of the treats in which Edinburgh folks delighted.

CHAPTER XII

FAILING HEALTH—DEATH

Poetical instincts—Religious views—Religious and emotional influences in his life—Doubts—Revivalism—Health—Overwork tells—Bed—Gradual failure—Death on May 6, 1870—Grave offered in Westminster Abbey—Buried at Warriston—Obituary notices—Bust in the Abbey—His greatness.

The emotional part of Sir James Simpson's nature found some small expression in versifying both, as we have seen, in early years and in later days. We know that he was a close student of Shakspeare, but Miss Simpson states that her father probably never entered a theatre, so that he can never have seen a representation. He was familiar with modern poets, especially with Burns. It is related that he once tested a lady friend's insight into the vernacular by quoting from memory for explanation the following lines from the national bard:—

"Baudrons sit by the ingle-neuk,
An' wi' her loof her face she's washin',
Willie's wife it nae sae trig,
She dichts her grunzie wi' a hooschen."

His own verses were neither better nor worse than those written by other men whose abilities have led them to excel in more practical pursuits. In youth they celebrated student life, or were, as usual, dedicated to Celia's eyebrows; in mature life they were of a more serious, and latterly of a strong religious description. At all times he delighted in writing little doggerel verses to his children or friends; valueless as such efforts are, they served a useful purpose; their composition was a recreation and pleasant relief to his over-taxed brain, while it was an amusement to him to watch their effect upon the recipients, and perhaps to receive a reply clothed also in the garb of rhyme.

Sir James's example so influenced the people amongst whom he lived that it is impossible to omit reference to his attitude throughout life towards religion and an account of what is one of the most interesting phases in his history. Up to Christmas, 1861, he had been, in the eyes of the religious public, an ordinary citizen; as regular in church-going as his professional engagements permitted; thoroughly interested in Church affairs, and a strong supporter of his own Church; possessing to the full the national characteristic of intimate acquaintance with the letter of the Old and New Testaments; and something of a theologian as well, as his answer to the religious objections to anæsthesia showed. At that period, to the delight of many, and the genuine astonishment of others among his fellow-citizens, he became a leading spirit in the strong Evangelical movement which was then spreading through the country, "Simpson is converted," cried the enthusiastic revivalist. "Simpson is converted now," laughed those who had opposed every action of his. "If Professor Simpson is converted, it is time some of the rest of us were seeing if we do not need to be converted," wisely answered one of his friends. In the ordinary sense of the word Simpson was not converted. Had he passed away without developing this latter-day Evangelical enthusiasm, all sects would still have united in thankfulness that such a man had lived. Why this religious revival during the sixties affected him as it did becomes evident in looking at the religious, moral, and emotional influences which affected him throughout his career.

The simple-minded, devout mother, strong in faith and strong in works, who passed out of his life when he was but nine years old, left a vivid impression on the boy's mind. In after years he would call up the picture of the good woman retiring from the shop and the worries and troubles of daily life into which she had so vigorously thrown herself and so bravely faced even with failing health, into the quiet little room behind, to kneel down in prayer; and would describe how at other times she went about her work chanting to herself one of the old Scots metrical psalms:

"Jehovah hear thee in the day, when trouble He did send
And let the name of Jacob's God thee from all ill defend.
Let Him remember all thy gifts, accept thy sacrifice,
Grant thee thine heart's wish and fulfil thy thoughts and counsel wise."

132

He used to relate one memory of her, touching in its simplicity: how one day he entered the house with a big hole in his stocking which she perceived and drew him on to her knee to darn. As she pulled the repaired garment on she said, "My Jamie, when your mother's away, you will mind that she was a grand darner." He remembered the words as if they had been spoken but yesterday, and subsequently offered to a lady who had established a girls' Industrial School in his native village a prize for the best darning.

The simple faith which beat in the life of the Bathgate baker's household was ingrained into James Simpson; he went forth into the world full of it, and full of the determination that by his fruits he should be known.

The tender, loving care for his welfare of his sisters and brothers, particularly of Sandy, who never faltered in his inspired belief in James's great future, kept alive in Simpson something of his mother's affectionate nature, and kindled the sympathies and emotions which bulked so large in his character. His goodness was displayed in his kindly treatment of the poor, who formed at first the whole and afterwards no small part of his patients. When name and fame and bread were his, he did not turn his back on the poor, but as we have seen, ever placed his skill at their disposal for no reward, as readily as he yielded it to the greatest in the land. As in his daily practice, so in his greatest professional efforts, the revelation of chloroform, the fight for anæsthesia, the introduction of acupressure, the crusade against hospitalism, one thought breathed through his work—that he might do something to better the condition of suffering humanity. He never attempted to keep discoveries in his own hands, to profit by the monopoly, but scattered wide the knowledge which had come to him that it might benefit mankind and grow stronger and wider in the hands of other workers.

In his domestic life he was a tender, loving, and companionable husband and father, a charming host, and a warm-hearted friend. "In this Edinburgh of ours," says a recent writer, "there are familiar faces whose expression changes greatly at the mention of his name; there are men whose speech from formal and precise turns headlong and extravagant, as if it came from a new and inspired vocabulary." In Scotland his personal influence was immense. As was afterwards written of him, "Great in his art, and peerless in

133

resource, yet greater was he in his own great soul;" such a man stood in no need of the violent revolution in mode of life implied in conversion. A gradual process of development led to his feeling that although to labour was to pray, there was a need for more attention to the spiritual, even in his self-sacrificing life.

There is evidence that during a brief period of his career Simpson became affected by speculative doubts; indeed it would have been surprising if his mind had not been affected by some of the new schools of thought which sprang up in the footsteps of Charles Darwin, and appeared for a time to threaten a mortal antagonism to all that was dear to orthodox Christians. But these did not influence him long; true to his character he examined every new thought and finding it wanting remained firm in his old and tried faith, and ranged himself on the side of those who perceived nothing seriously incompatible between religion and modern science.

In his bearing, when the angel of sorrow afflicted his household with no unsparing hand, we find him always a religious-minded man. The first trial was the loss of the eldest child, his daughter Maggie, in 1844. Another daughter, Mary, was lost in early infancy. In 1848 his friend of boyhood and student days, Professor John Reid, was smitten with a painful malady and died after a prolonged period of suffering during which, knowing that the shadow of death was hanging over him, he devoted himself in retirement to religious thoughts. Experiences such as these made Simpson pause and question himself. Brimful of life and vigour, however much he came in contact with death in his professional rounds, the sight of it in his own inner circle powerfully stirred his emotional nature. His friend the Rev. Dr. Duns noticed in him after these sad events a gradually increasing earnestness in his spiritual life, and a closer inquiry into the meanings of the Scriptures. He sought out the company, and placed himself under the influence of those among his patients whom he knew to possess fervid religious temperaments. The last mental stumbling-block was the question of prayer; he had seriously doubted in examining the question intellectually that human prayer could influence the purpose of the Deity. It is difficult, if not presumptuous, to inquire into the process whereby, under the guidance of spiritually minded friends, his doubts were satisfied.

"... One indeed I knew

In many a subtle question versed."
"He fought his doubts and gathered strength,
He would not make his judgment blind,
He faced the spectres of the mind,
And laid them—thus he came at length"
"To find a stronger faith his own."

The simple earnest faith of his fathers in which he had commenced life, ran all through his mature years and prompted his strong purposeful energies. After the combat with the only seriously perplexing doubt he re-embraced his faith with the simplicity of a child and the strength of a giant. For one accustomed to apply to every subject taken in hand the rigid process of careful scientific investigation, it required no small effort to lay aside his usual methods and suffer himself to be led wholly by faith.

It was impossible for Simpson to enter into any movement without taking a prominent part in it. That Christmas Day on which all doubts left him was followed by days of extraordinarily zealous work, such as would have been expected of him after he had convinced himself that he had a mission to spread abroad this, the latest, and, in his opinion, the greatest, of his discoveries. He plunged at once into the midst of Evangelical societies, missions, and prayer-meetings, amongst the upper and lower classes of Edinburgh, and made excursions into the mining districts of his native county to deliver addresses. He interested himself in the education of theological students, and in foreign missions, and added to his literary work the writing of religious addresses, tracts and hymns. His example had a powerful influence in Edinburgh. It is said that he frequently addressed on a Sunday evening Evangelical assemblies of two thousand persons. The news of his so-called conversion was gleefully spread by well-meaning folks, who had given credence to statements published by his enemies, and imagined that here was a bad if a great man turned aside from the broad to the narrow path. This enthusiastic revival movement died down in time, and Simpson returned to his ordinary everyday life.

More sorrow soon fell to his lot. In 1862 his fifth child, James, who had always been an invalid, was taken from him at the age of fifteen. In 1866 the sad death of Dr. David Simpson, the eldest son, which has already been referred to, was followed in about a month's time by that of the eldest surviving daughter, Jessie, at the age of seventeen. The death of James, a sweet-natured child, stimulated him in the revival work. Pious friends had surrounded the little sufferer and led him to add his innocent influence in exciting his father's religious emotions.

There is reason to believe that Simpson perceived much insincerity in the revival movement, and attempted to dissociate himself from active participation in it, on account of finding it impossible to work in harmony with some who, though loud in profession, flagrantly failed in practice.

The subject of Simpson's health has been little referred to in these pages, because throughout his life he paid little attention to it. The chief remedy for the feeling of indisposition was change of work. He found it impossible to be idle, and sought as recreation occupations such as archæological research, or a scamper round foreign hospitals, which to most people would have savoured more of labour. The part of his body which was most worked, his nervous system, was naturally the one which most often troubled him with disorder; like other great men of high mental development he suffered from time to time with severe attacks of megrim, which necessitated a few hours of rest. The blood-poisoning, for which he availed himself of Professor Syme's services, was soon recovered from with prompt treatment ending in a foreign tour; but after it little illnesses became more frequent, and he was perforce occasionally confined to the house. During these times he busied himself, for the sake of occupation and to distract his attention from his sufferings, in professional reading or the preparation of literary papers. Rheumatic troubles became frequent, and soon after his eldest son's death he had to run over to the Isle of Man to free himself from a severe attack of sciatica.

Long, weary nights spent at the bedside of patients or in tiresome railway journeys, and exposure to all varieties of weather, had a serious effect upon him. Travelling was slow, according to modern ideas, and long waits at wayside stations in winter-time helped to play havoc with his constitution. He was well known to the railway officials in Scotland. The figure of the great Edinburgh professor was familiar at many a station, striding up and down the platform with the stationmaster, chaffing the porter, or cheerily chatting to the driver and stoker leaning out of the engine. After his death many of these men would proudly produce little mementoes of their services to him, which he never forgot to send.

The little rest house, Viewbank, on the Forth, had to be more frequently sought refuge in, if only to get away from the harassing night-bell and secure a full night's sleep. In the last year or two of his existence he found the work of his practice and chair hard to carry on, not because of any defined illness, but on account of the loss of that buoyant elasticity of constitution which had enabled him to bear without apparent effort or injury the fatigue which would have been sufficient to prostrate more than one ordinary man. He had early trained himself to do with a minimum of sleep; to snatch what he could and when he could, if it were only on a sofa, a bare board, or in one of the comfortless railway carriages of the day. He took full advantage during his career of the modern facilities for travelling which he had seen introduced and developed. Many a night was spent in the train, going to or returning from a far-distant patient, or after a combined professional and archæological excursion; the next morning would find him busy in his usual routine. On the day after receiving the degree of D.C.L. at Oxford in 1866, he started for Devizes, which was reached the same evening; here he had a hasty meal and drove on to Avebury to see the standing stones there. He returned at midnight, and at five o'clock next morning set off for Stonehenge, a place he had long desired to see, thoroughly examined the remarkable remains, and on his return took train to Bath, where he found time to examine more antiquities. At midnight a telegram reached him calling him professionally to Northumberland. He snatched a few hours' sleep, and taking the four a.m. train to London set out for Northumberland, where he saw his patient, and then proceeded to Edinburgh. This is no solitary instance of his journeyings, but an example of many.

When the year 1870 had been entered upon, he awoke to the fact that his flesh was too weak for his eager spirit; despite this, he held on his course, and worked without ceasing, never refusing an urgent call, although he now suffered from angina pectoris. On February 12th he hastened to London to give evidence in a notorious divorce case. He arrived only to find that the trial had been postponed for four days. He returned to Edinburgh on the 14th, spent the next day in professional visits in the country, and arrived again in London in time to appear in the witness-box on the 16th, although chilled to the bone by the coldness of the long journey. On the following day he stopped at York on his way home, dined with Lord Houghton, and visited, at 11 p.m., his friend Dr. Williams, in Micklegate. During the remainder of the journey from York to Edinburgh he suffered severely, and "was glad to rest for awhile upon the floor of the railway carriage."

A few days after this last run to London he was summoned to see a patient in Perth, but was this time so fatigued by the effort, that after his return on February 25th he was obliged to take to bed. The news sped to all quarters of the globe that Simpson was gravely ill, for nothing but grave illness could compel that vigorous man to completely lay down his work.

His symptoms improved at first under appropriate treatment sufficiently to allow him to be placed on a bed in the drawing-room; and he even once more took up his favourite archæology, revising some of his work in that subject. Patients also were not to be denied; many were seen and prescribed for in his sick room, some even being carried up to his presence. But the fatal disease regained ascendancy, and the fact became apparent to all, not excepting himself, that the last chapter of the closely written book of his life had been entered upon. Towards the end of March, by his own request, his eldest surviving son was telegraphed for to be near him, and he wrote a touching letter to his youngest son, then a student in Geneva, encouraging him in his studies, asking him to look for cup-markings cut in the curious islet rock in Lake Geneva, and ending with an expression of his feeling of impending death, for which he felt perfectly and happily prepared. In these last days he loved to have his nearest and dearest around him; Lady Simpson and others read to him, and his daughter tells us how she daily prepared her school lessons in the sick room with his help; to the last he interested himself in the work of his relations and friends. He answered the attack of Bigelow, of Boston, conscious that it was his last effort on behalf of chloroform, and wrote to all his old opponents asking their forgiveness if at any time words of his had wounded their feelings. He might well have spared himself the regrets—such as they were—which troubled him. "I would have liked to have completed hospitalism," he said, "but I hope some good man will take it up." On another occasion he asked, "How old am I? Fifty-nine? Well, I have done some work. I wish I had been busier."

He expressed a desire that his nephew should succeed him in the Chair of Midwifery—he would, he thought, help to perpetuate his treatment.

There was much communing with himself on his future, and all his sayings on the subject breathed the simple faith first inculcated in him in the Bathgate cottage. His great sufferings, sometimes allayed by opiates and his own chloroform, were bravely borne, but the days dragged sadly on. On the evening of May 5th Sandy took his place at his side, and the last conscious moments of the great physician were spent with his head in the arms of him who had helped and guided him through the difficult days of his career. At sunset on May 6th he passed peacefully away.

The extent of the feeling evoked by the tidings of his death was represented in Mr. Gladstone's remark that it was a grievous loss to the nation and was truly a national concern. There was a universally expressed opinion that he merited without a shadow of doubt the rare national honour of public interment in Westminster Abbey. A committee was formed out of the leading medical men in London to carry out this suggestion. Their task was light, for the Dean acceded to the request at once. Much as his family and the Scots people valued this tribute to his greatness, they decided otherwise. Scotland has no counterpart of Westminster in which to lay to rest those whom she feels to have been her greatest; but Edinburgh felt that she could not part with him who in life had been her possession and her pride. He had long ago chosen a piece of ground in the Warriston cemetery, and Lady Simpson decided, to the gratification of his fellow-citizens, that he should be buried there beside the five children who had preceded him. His resting place was well chosen; it nestled into the side of the beautiful city, and from it could be viewed some of the chief objects of the scene he knew so well—on the south the stately rock crowned with the ancient castle, and the towering flats of the old town stretching away to Arthur's Seat; on the north the long stretch of the Firth of Forth and in the distance on the one hand the

Ochills; on the other the Bass Rock.

The funeral was one of the most remarkable ever witnessed in Scotland. It took place on May 13th in the presence of a crowd estimated to consist of thirty thousand persons. The hearse was followed by a representative procession comprising close upon two thousand persons. His own relatives assembled at 52, Queen Street, the general public and the Town Council in the Free Church of St. Luke, and the representatives of the University, the Colleges of Physicians and Surgeons, and the Royal Society and many other public bodies, in the Hall of the College of Physicians. At each of these meeting-places religious services were held. The whole city ceased to labour that afternoon in order to pay the last tribute to its dearly loved professor. The poor mourned in the crowd as deeply and genuinely as those with whom he had been closely associated in life mourned as they followed his remains in the procession. Every mourner grieved from a sense of personal loss, so deeply had his influence sunk down into the hearts of the people.

The companion of his troubles and his triumphs, who had bravely joined him to help him to the fame he strove after, was soon laid beside him. Lady Simpson died on June 17th of the same year.

But two notes were struck in the countless obituary notices and letters of condolence which appeared from far and near—those of appreciation of his great nature, and sorrow for the terrible loss sustained by science and humanity. The Queen caused the Duke of Argyle to express to the family her own personal sorrow at the loss of "so great and good a man." A largely attended meeting was held in Washington to express the feeling of his own profession in the United States, at which Dr. Storer moved, "that in Dr. Simpson, American physicians recognise not merely an eminent and learned Scots practitioner, but a philanthropist whose love encircled the world; a discoverer who sought and found for suffering humanity in its sorest need a foretaste of the peace of heaven, and a devoted disciple of the only true physician, our Saviour Jesus Christ."

The following original verses from the pen of a well-known scholar in

the profession, were given prominence in the columns of the *Lancet*:—
PROMETHEUS.

(Our lamented Sir James Simpson was the subject of angina pectoris.)

1

"Alas! alas! pain, pain, ever forever!"
So groaned upon his rock that Titan good
Who by his brave and loving hardihood
Was to weak man of priceless boons the giver,
Which e'en the supreme tyrant could not sever
From us, once given; we own him in our food
And in our blazing hearth's beatitude;
Yet still his cry was "Pain, ever forever!"
Shall we a later, harder doom rehearse?
One came whose art men's dread of are repressed:
Mangled and writhing limb he lulled to rest,
And stingless left the old Semitic curse;
Him, too, for these blest gifts did Zeus amerce?
He, too, had vultures tearing at his breast.
2

Hush, Pagan plaints! our Titan is unbound;
The cruel beak and talons scared away;
As once upon his mother's lap he lay
So rests his head august on holy ground;
Spells stronger than his own his pangs have found;
He hears no clamour of polemic fray,
Nor reeks he what unthankful men may say;
Nothing can vex him in that peace profound.

And where his loving soul, his genius bold?
In slumber? or already sent abroad
On angels' wings and works, as some men hold?
Or waiting Evolution's change, unawed?
All is a mystery, as Saint Paul has told,
Saying, "Your life is hid with Christ in God."

In a peaceful corner of the St. Andrew Chapel in Westminster Abbey, alongside memorials of Sir Humphry Davy and a few other scientists of note, stands a speaking image in marble—perhaps the most expressive representation that exists—of this wonderful man,

"To whose genius and benevolence

The world owes the blessings derived

From the use of chloroform for

The relief of suffering.

Laus Deo."

Mr. Jonathan Hutchinson, when writing to the medical journals in support of the proposal to secure Simpson's burial in Westminster Abbey, foretold that his reputation would ripen with years, that jealousies would be forgotten, and antagonism would be buried. Twenty-seven years have elapsed since then, and few remain with whom he came in conflict; those who do remain exchanged, along with others of his opponents, friendly words of reconciliation in the end, and took the hand which he held out from his deathbed. As a man, Simpson had his faults; but they were exaggerated in his lifetime by some, just as his capabilities and achievements were magnified by those who worshipped him as inspired. He was full of sympathy for mankind, benevolent and honest to a fault, and forbearing to his enemies. He rushed eagerly into the combat and oftentimes wounded sorely, and perhaps unnecessarily. His genius was essentially a reforming genius, and impelled him to fight for his ends, for genius is always the "master of man." We can forgive him if sometimes it caused him to fight too vigorously, where the heart of a man of mere talent might have failed and lost. His social charms were excelled only by his marvellous energy, his prodigious memory, and his keenness of insight; but he was regrettably inattentive to the details of ordinary everyday life and practice.

He approached the study of medicine when the darkness of the Middle Ages was still upon it, and was one of the first to point out that although many diseases appeared incurable, they were nevertheless preventable. Although no brilliant operator himself, he so transformed the surgical theatre by his revelation of the power of chloroform, and by his powerful advocacy of the use of anæsthetics, that pain was shut out and vast scientific possibilities opened up; many of which have been brilliantly realised by subsequent workers. He devoted himself specially to the despised obstetric art, fighting for what he recognised as the most lowly and neglected branch of his profession, ranging his powerful forces on the side of the weak, and left it the most nearly perfect of medical sciences.

He was enthusiastic in his belief in progress, and in the power of steady, honest work to effect great ends. With the exception of the time of that temporary burst into revivalism in 1861, his motto throughout life might very well have been *laborare est orare*. He was no believer in speculations, but curiously enough kept for recreation only the subject of archæology, in which he entered into many intricate speculative studies. In his professional work he avoided speculation, and never adopted a theory which was not built upon firm fact.

If we are asked for what we are most to honour Simpson, we answer, not so much for the discoveries he made, not for the instruments he invented, not for his exposure of numerous evils, not for the introduction of reforms, not for any particular contribution to science, literature, or archæology; but rather for the inspiring life of the man looked at both in outline and in detail. He was guided by high ideals, and a joyous unhesitating belief that all good things were possible—that right must prevail. He was stimulated by a genius which, as has been pointed out, gave him the energy to fight for his ends with herculean strength. The fact that chloroform was by his efforts alone accepted as *the* anæsthetic, and ether, which from the first was generally thought to be safer in ordinary hands, was deliberately put on one side practically all over the world, testified to his forcible and convincing method, and to his power of making others see as he saw. As a man of science alone, as a philanthropist alone, as a worker alone, as a reformer alone, he was great. But although to the popular mind he is known chiefly

144

because of his introduction of chloroform, medical history will record him as greater because of his reforming genius, and will point to the fight for anæsthesia, and his crusade against hospitalism as the best of all that he accomplished or initiated. And he who, while making allowances for the weaknesses of human nature which were Simpson's, studies the life which was brought all too soon to a close, will recognise the great spirit which breathed through all his life.

THE END.

APPENDIX

I.

The following is a list of Sir James Simpson's contributions to *Archæology*. His professional writings, in the form of contributions to the medical journals, or of papers read to various societies or meetings, number close upon two hundred.

1. "Antiquarian Notices of Leprosy and Leper Hospitals in Scotland and England." (Three papers read before the Medico-Chirurgical Society, March 3, 1841.) *Edinburgh Medical and Surgical Journal*, October, 1841, and January and April, 1842.

2. "Notice of Roman Practitioner's Medicine Stamp found near Tranent." Royal Society of Edinburgh; Dec. 16, 1850.

3. "Ancient Roman Medical Stamps." *Edinburgh Journal of Medical Science*, Jan., March, April, 1851.

4. "Was the Roman Army provided with any Medical Officers?" Edinburgh, 1851, private circulation.

5. "Notes on some Ancient Greek Medical Vases for containing Lykion; and on the modern use of the same in India." Edinburgh, 1856.

6. "Notice of the appearance of Syphilis in Scotland in the last years of the fifteenth century." 1860.

7. "Note on a Pictish Inscription in the Churchyard of St. Vigeans." Royal Society, April 6, 1863.

8. "Notes on some Scottish Magical Charm-Stones or Curing Stones." *Proceedings of Antiquarian Society of Scotland*, vol iv., 1868.

9. "An Account of two Barrows at Spottiswoode, Berwickshire, opened by the Lady John Scott." *Proceedings of Antiquarian Society of Scotland*, vol iv., 1868.

10. "Did John de Vigo describe Acupressure in the Sixteenth Century?" *British Medical Journal*, Aug. 24, 1867; *Medical Times and Gazette*, 1867, vol. ii., p. 187.

11. "Account of some Ancient Sculptures on the Walls of Caves in Fife." 1867.

12. "Notices of some Ancient Sculptures on the Walls of Caves." *Proceedings of the Royal Society*; Edinburgh, 1867.

13. "Cup-cuttings and Ring-cuttings on the Calder Stones, near Liverpool." 1866. *Transactions of the Historical Society of Lancashire and Cheshire.*

14. "Archæology—its past and its future work." Annual Address to the Society of Antiquarians of Scotland, January 28, 1861.

15. "The Cat Stane, Edinburghshire." *Proceedings of the Society of Antiquaries, Scotland*, 1861.

16. "Archaic Sculpturings of Cups, Circles, &c., upon Stones and Rocks in Scotland, England, and other countries." 1867.

17. "Is the Pyramid at Gizeh a Meteorological Monument?" *Proceedings of the Royal Society*; Edinburgh, 1868.

18. "Pyramidal Structures in Egypt and elsewhere." *Proceedings of the Royal Society*; Edinburgh, 1868.

19. "Cell at Inchcolm."

The above list is founded on that given by Professor Gusscrow in his "Zur Erinnerung an Sir James Y. Simpson." Berlin, 1871.

II.

On *post mortem* examination the following observations on Sir James Simpson's head were made:—

Skull —circumference round by occipital protuberance and below frontal eminences, 22½ inches. —from ear to ear, 13 inches. —from occipital protuberance to point between superciliary ridges, 13 inches. *Brain* —weight of entire brain (cerebrum and cerebellum) was 54 ounces; the cerebellum, pons, and medulla oblongata weighed 5¼ ounces. The convolutions of the cerebrum were remarkable for their number, depth, and intricate foldings. This was noticed more particularly in the anterior lobes and the islands of Reil.

Extract from *British Medical Journal*, May 14, 1870.